Lansing High School

The Oracle

Lansing High School

The Oracle

ISBN/EAN: 9783337367725

Printed in Europe, USA, Canada, Australia, Japan

Cover: Foto ©Andreas Hilbeck / pixelio.de

More available books at **www.hansebooks.com**

E. LEO DI MAZZINI

A. M., M. D., Ph. D., D. Lit. and Sci.

Fellow of Trinity School

Ex-Professor of Chemistry, Donington College

Specialist in Chronic Diseases—Bright's, Diabetes, Rheumatism, Paralysis, Dropsy and Cancer.

Office, 323 Washington Ave. S.   Residence, 511 Washington Ave. S.

"When may I sleep again?" he cried,
As the baby began to squall,
And a saucy echo answered back,
"After the bawl."— *Ex.*

"May I print a kiss on your cheek?"
I asked. She nodded sweet permission;
So we went to press, and I rather guess
I printed a large edition. *Ex.*

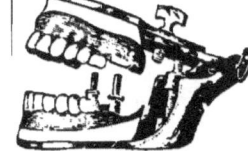

The only way a man can win an argument with a woman is to state his side of the case and walk away. —Ex.

You can hardly expect a young man to make any progress with his first moustache when everybody takes delight in calling it down.—Ex.

There must be a woman in the moon instead of a man, otherwise it wouldn't change so often. Ex.

When a married man has his hair cut, his wife loses her strongest hold on him. Ex.

The fresh half-sole that a mother applies to her offspring's trousers contradicts the theory that there is nothing new under the son. -Ex.

PROFESSIONAL DIRECTORY

Bobby's mother had been trying to show him that he must speak respectfully of older people.

Bobby (at night) "Father, what are the two parties in the legislature?"

FATHER (reading) "Pingree and anti-Pingree."

TEACHER (at morning) "Bobby, what parties are most powerful in the legislature?"

Bobby "Uncle Pingree and Auntie Pingree."

Even the oldest inhabitant never saw a negro and a brass band going in opposite directions. *Ex.*

Some men are like dice easily rattled, but hard to shake. *Ex.*

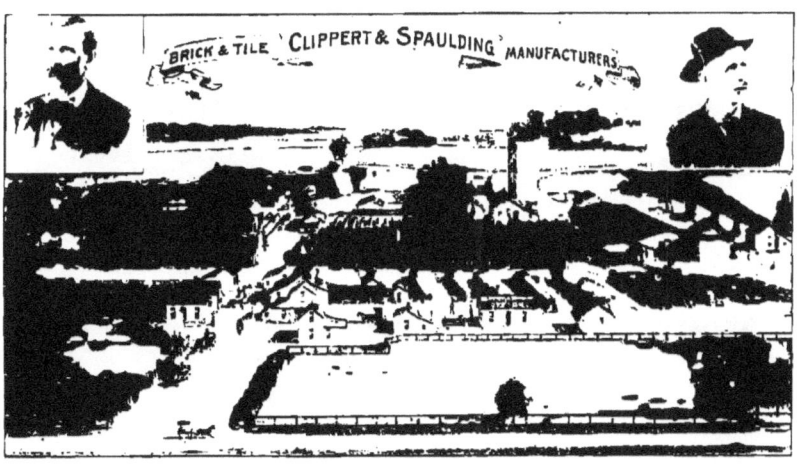

It is strange but true that the lungs of a dog are the seat of his pants. *Ex.*

Whenever a doctor dies an undertaker loses his best friend. *Ex.*

Heat travels faster than cold—anyone can catch cold. *Ex.*

The turtle may be slow, but he usually gets there in time for the soup.—*Ex.*

It never occurs to a boy that he will sometime know as little as his father.—*Ex.*

Woman's success as an engineer is phenomenal. She frequently has a wash-out on the line, but no disasters are recorded. *Ex.*

There is always room at the bottom—of an early strawberry box.—*Ex.*

The darkest hour is always when you can't find the matches. *Ex.*

Men may come and men may go, but the gas meter goes on forever. *Ex.*

It's a wise father that knows as much as his own son. *Ex.*

It is always surprising how much deeper a hole is after you get into it.--*Ex.*

When the devil goes fishing for men, he baits his hook with a pretty woman.—*Ex.*

The usual board of arbitration between a bad boy and his father consists of a shingle. *Ex.*

Large Reward Offered for the Below Named Articles

A vase for the flower of the family.
Lining from a coverlid of snow.
Fringe from the mantle of charity.
Someone to answer the letters of the alphabet.
The key to the vault of the sky.
A pencil with which to write on the tablets given by physicians.
A gown to match the sashes of windows.
The stem of the leaf of a book.
Spectacles to fit the eyes of a potato.
The palm tree which grows the dates on the calendar.
Cloth made from the silk on corn.
A sleigh with runners of strawberries.
A parrot which will eat the cracker on a whip.
A preparation to clean the spots from the sun.
Some way to untie the knots in wood.
The arrows that go with the bows of spectacles.

Spokes from the wheel of fortune.
The bell which rings the peel of an onion.
Feathers from the tick of a clock.
Flour made from the grain of wood.
Something to disturb the nap of velvet.
An agent for the polish of education.
A machine to utilize the energy caused by the fall of pride.
A knife to sharpen the point of a joke.
A hat to fit the head of a drum.
A bank to cash the check in gingham.
Pigs kept in a gold pen.
Foliage from an electric plant.
Something to take the curl out of smoke.
The tune played on the horns of the moon.
A package tied with the strings on beans.
A bird with a ten-dollar bill.
The locks that go with the Florida Keys.
A lawn sprinkled with a spray of flowers.
A ship which can ride the waves in a young lady's hair.

Dedication

LANSING HIGH SCHOOL BUILDING.

Lansing High School

COLORS

Red and White

SCHOOL YELL

Ooh Rah! Ooh Rah!
Wah, Pah, Sah!
Lansing High School,
Rah! Rah! Rah!

Introduction

With the title of Senior of the High School we inherited the publication of the ORACLE. As a consequence of too lofty aspirations on the part of previous editors, to make each ORACLE more attractive than the last, there was an unpleasant feature of this heritage. It was not alone the result of the failure of last year's class to meet their financial obligations, but the storm had been slowly gathering for several years and it was our fortune or misfortune, whichever you choose, to have this cloudburst fall upon us.

When our thoughts turned for the first time toward this enterprise and the word ORACLE was heard again in school, we were called up on the carpet before the stern brow of the faculty and informed that there were a few things we must not do, chief among which was that of incurring more expense than we could meet. We agreed to the suggestion, thinking discretion the better part of valor, outwardly longing to clothe '99 in a better dress than '98 and inwardly rejoicing at this opportunity of laying any criticism we may arouse upon the broad shoulders of the faculty.

It is our sincere hope that you will find in this volume something more than a fine display or expensive cover. We have tried to make it interesting and amusing, and to give you a true insight into the High School life as it is.

We who have been entrusted with this work have put forth the best effort consistent with our other school duties. In its preparation we we have been prompted by none but the best impulses toward our school. We feel, however, that it is our duty to show forth things as they appear to us. But, believe us, if we do show forth any peculiarity, it does not arise from a spirit of personal injury; it is merely voicing the opinions of the High School students as we know them. We wish our classmates to see themselves as others see them and as they see others.

If by chance we should be so unfortunate as to displease any one, do not wreak your vengeance upon us. Remember that "There are always two Johns —John's John, and Thomas' John," and that our descriptions are given from our view of the sign board. Scan them, then, in a forgiving spirit, for from our standpoint you may gain a broader view.

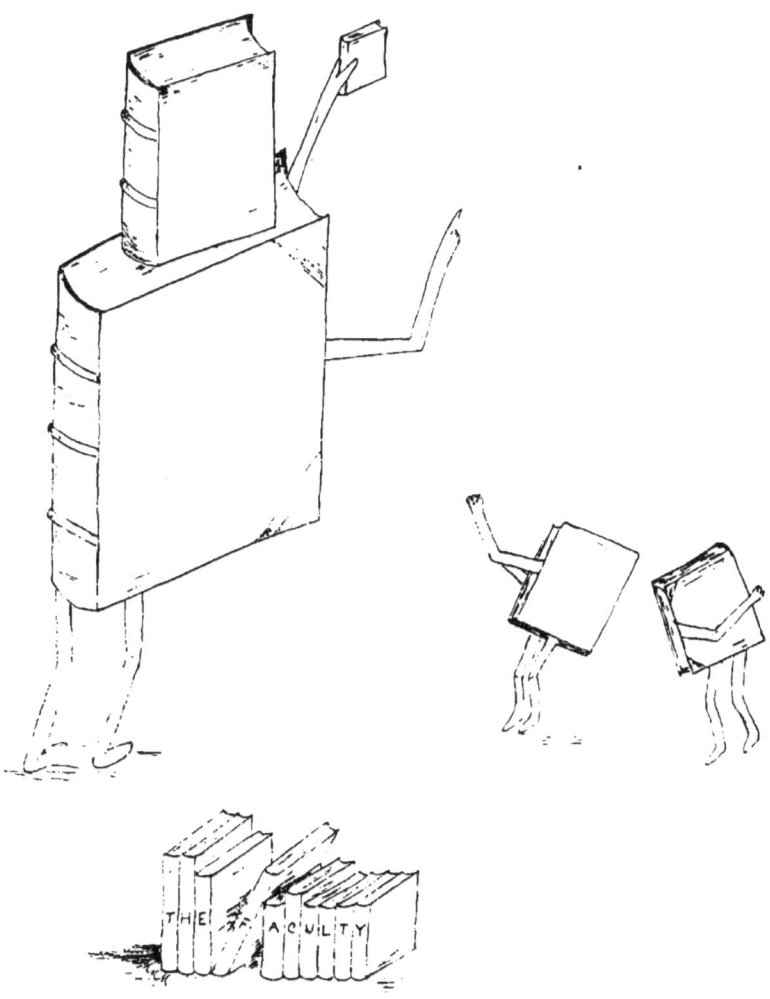

THE FACULTY

B

Faculty

CLARENCE E. HOLMES, Principal, 218 Seymour St.
Geometry, Geology, Botany.

CHRISTINE F. BRONSON, Assistant Principal, 313 Shiawassee W.,
Latin.

HELEN DOUGLAS, 412 Michigan Ave. W.,
General History, U. S. History, Political Economy.

VERNON J. WILLEY, Chestnut St. S.,
Physics, Chemistry.

GRACE M. SMITH, 212 Saginaw St. W.,
History, English.

EDITH E. ATKINS, 604 Michigan Ave. W.,
Latin, Greek.

EMMA A. LOTT, 214 Chestnut St. N.,
Physiology, English.

IDA A. LAMB, 313 Shiawassee St. W.,
German.

ERNESTINE P. ROBINSON, 204 Willow St.,
English Literature.

H. MELVA KING, 415 Washington Ave. N.,
Algebra, English.

ALICE CARRIER, 516 Ionia St. W.,
Botany, U. S. History.

GUY D. SMITH, 311 Hillsdale St. W.,
Algebra, Arithmetic.

THE FACULTY

Helen Douglas

Miss Helen Douglas, teacher of United States, English and General History, was born in Ann Arbor. Here she attended the public schools, from which she was graduated in 1892. She also attended the University there, and completed her course in 1896 with a degree of Ph. B.

She then accepted a position as teacher of General History in Three Rivers, which she held until last spring, when she accepted the position offered her in our school.

Miss Douglas' work has been very satisfactory, and she will remain with us next year.

Vernon J. Willey

Vernon J. Willey was born and brought up on a farm near Pewamo, Ionia County. He attended district school until fifteen years of age, when he entered the Pewamo High School, continuing there until 1887, and finishing his High School work one year later at the Portland High School.

After teaching one year in a district school he entered the Michigan Agricultural College in September, 1889, and taught a winter term of district school each year of his college course.

After his graduation in 1893, Mr. Willey was appointed Principal of the Michigan School for the Blind, where he remained as teacher of Science and Mathematics until he began his work as science teacher in the Lansing High School in November, 1898.

Grace Smith

Miss Grace Smith was born and brought up in Saline, Washtenaw County. Here she attended the public school and graduated from the High School. The next year she entered the Ypsilanti Normal School. After graduating from the Normal she taught three years in the Manchester High School. She next took a course at the University of Michigan, completing it in 1897.

Last year she accepted a position as teacher of English and History in the Caro High School, but gave it up at the end of her first year in order to accept a position as teacher of the same studies in the Lansing High School.

Guy D. Smith

Guy D. Smith was born on a farm one mile south of Mason. He attended a district school until eleven years of age, when he entered the Mason city school, from which he graduated at the age of seventeen.

The next three years of his life were spent teaching school winters and working on his father's farm summers.

In 1894 he entered Kalamazoo College and, working his way through college by tutoring and various other kinds of work, was graduated in 1898 with a degree of A. B.

Mr. Smith was quite prominent in college, being a member of the college ball team for four years and of the foot ball team for three years, besides being President of his class two consecutive terms, president of Sherwood Rhetorical Society and president of the college Y. M. C. A. for two years.

After graduating Mr. Smith accepted a position in our school, where he has charge of the ninth grade assembly room.

Ernestine Robinson

Miss Ernestine Robinson was born in Central New York, where she lived till she was eight years old, when she moved to this city. She attended the public school here and is a graduate of the Lansing High School.

In 1892 Miss Robinson entered the Kansas State University, where she remained one year. entering Ann Arbor as a Sophomore in '93, where she graduated with high honors in '96. While here she became a member of the Kappa Kappa Gamma Fraternity.

After leaving the University she accepted a position as teacher of English Literature in the High School at Sault Ste. Marie. She held this position for two years, giving it up in '98 to accept a similar position in our school, which she is filling very satisfactorily.

Board of Education

Song of a Knife

I.

Lives of students all remind us
   There are marks made not by feet;
We, departing, leave behind us
   Marks upon each High School seat.

II.

Knife-marks which I doubt not others
   Gazing on each dark ink-stain-
Thoughtless and misguided brothers—
   Seeing may cut more again.

III.

Life is short; man's devastation
   Kills the forest; carve no more
Lest the coming generation
   Sit upon the High School floor!

IV.

Art? 'Tis not by any token.
   Stay the devastating tool,
"Make your mark" was never spoken
   Of the marks on seats in school.

            —M. M. M.

Editorials

We have attempted to make the ORACLE of this year a school and not a class publication. Although we have not perfected our scheme yet, we have gone far enough to see its benefits. It is our sincere hope that this method will be adopted by our successors, for there is no reason why one class should have entire control of the only paper in the High School. The ORACLE has previously been of most value to the Senior class. We hope to make it equally valuable to all classes. If all were united in this work, and each made to feel that they have a part to perform, the ORACLE would become a better representative of the school.

It is our plan to give each class two representatives, who shall have equal power with the Senior board. These representatives are to have four assistants, to meet with them, and the six constitute a board to have charge of the work in each class. There are many advantages in this system, which can be readily seen. The one of most use to the High School is that of giving experience to those who are to take charge of the paper in the future. It has been the regret of each board not to have a chance of applying the experience gained in trying again. We think this will give the desired opportunity.

*

The drawings of this year are from the pens of Miss Lillian Renner, Miss Mildred Moon and Miss Kate Ostrander. These drawings, although not very numerous, take no small amount of time and labor, and we desire to thank those who have so faithfully performed this task for us.

We desire to call attention to our advertisers. It is our request that the students and friends of the ORACLE patronize those who have thus favored us. When trading, please mention the ORACLE; it will show business men that their advertisements are noticed, and thereby greatly aid future ORACLE boards.

&

We extend our thanks to those classes who have so kindly assisted us in our final exit. The decorations for class day and commencement were certainly worthy of the highest praise, and bore unmistakable evidences of kindly hands.

&

The seven-hour method adopted last year as a substitute for the one-session plan has been continued during this year. Next to one session, this system is the best that could be employed. It enables the Seniors and others, who can so arrange their work, to be excused during the hot hours of the long summer afternoons.

&

Although the Athletic Association has been almost entirely in the hands of new men this year, yet it has prospered and is still free from debt, even though it has had obligations to meet for both the foot ball and base ball teams. We hope that now it has a start in the right direction, it will continue to prosper.

&

The photographs of this ORACLE were made by the Le Clear Photograph Co. We take this opportunity of acknowledging the extra care and untiring patience of the photographer, who more than fulfilled the qualifications of the contract. We have no hesitation in recommending him for future ORACLE work.

Owing to some circumstance which we are not able to account for, the proceeds of our Junior exhibition were not as much as we expected; therefore, our class was unable to help us financially, as they might otherwise have done. Nevertheless, they have given us the best support they were able, and we undoubtedly owe much of our success to this fact.

We feel, however, that certain members of the class must be criticised for their utter lack of any responsibility in regard to class affairs. This carelessness has its effect on other members of the class, and soon the class spirit is ready to have its grave strewn with forget-me-nots. This absence of class spirit has made it very difficult for class officers. We hope '00 will not be afflicted thus.

Dedicated to the Senior Boys—'99

(If the coat doesn't fit, don't put it on.)

We've got the *slowest* boys, their name is legion;
They're just the dullest things about the region.
There's something 'bout the crowd
That makes you sigh out loud;
"There's nothing 'bout these boys that's with the times."

You've heard, I think, of boys whose brains were many;
You've heard of those, I think, who haven't any;
    They're not in it with the '99's.
When to *parties* they have gone,
The girls go home alone!
    You'll surely know the fellows by *these* signs.

Oracle Board

Editor-in-Chief, CLARK JAGGER
Assistant Editor, MARIAN SEELEY
Business Manager, HERBERT BARRINGER
Advertising Manager, HAROLD HEDGES

Associate Editors

JESSIE LAIRD, CLARA ARMSTRONG, FRANC BENNETT, ARTHUR REASONER

ORACLE BOARD.
HERBERT BARRINGER   HAROLD HEDGES
ARTHUR REINONSEN   MARIAN SEELEY   JESSIE LAIRD
CLARA ARMSTRONG   CLARK JAGGER
LILLIAN RENSSEN   FRANC BENNETT

CLARA ARMSTRONG. "A maiden never bold, of spirit so still and quiet, that her motion blushes at herself." Entered the L. H. S. in 1895; Color Committee; Sophomore Exhibition; Secretary '97, '98; Junior X Committee; Oracle Board.

ADELBERT BAKER. "I grant you he is a little too good-natured." Entered the L. H. S. in 1894. On Base Ball Team '98 and '99.

AUSTIN BRANT. "Greater men than myself may have lived, but I doubt it." Entered L. H. S. in 1896. Sophomore Exhibition; Junior X; Treasurer 98, '99; Foot Ball Team '99; Board of Directors of A. A. '99; Banquet Committee.

HERBERT BARRINGER. "Deep on his front engraven deliberation sat, and public care." Entered the L. H. S. in 1895. Junior X Committee; Foot Ball Team '98, '99; Vice President A. A. '99; Business Manager of the ORACLE.

MOLLIE BUTTS. "In arguing, too, the person owned her skill
                For e'en though vanquished she could argue still."
Entered the L. H. S. in 1895.

OLIVE BRISBIN. "To be merry best becomes you, for out of all question you were born in a merry hour." Entered the L. H. S. in 1893; Junior X; Vice President '99. Chairman of Class Day Committee.

FRANC BENNETT. "I can not learn the mystery of awaking." Entered the L. H. S. in 1895. Color Committee. Sophomore Exhibition Committee. Vice President '97, '98; Junior Exhibition Committee; Pin Committee; Oracle Board.

CONSTANCE BEMENT. "Under her feet the grass grew green." Entered the L. H. S. in 1895; Finance Committee; Sophomore and Junior Decorating Committee; Senior Reception Committee: Class Prophetess.

NORA BAIRD. "The bright black eye, the melting blue,
She can not choose between the two.
But that is dearest all the while
Which wears for her the sweetest smile."
Entered the L. H. S. in 1895; Sophomore Exhibition; Sophomore Decorating Committee: Observer Board: Junior X Committee; Junior X.

JESSIE BIRD. "Thy soul was like a star and dwelt apart." Entered the L. H. S. in 1893.

THERON CHASE. "Strong of his hands, and strong on his legs, but still of his tongue." Entered the L. H. S. in 1895.

BELLE CADY. "The doctors are our friends, let 's use them well, for though they kill but slow they 're certain." Entered the L. H S. in 1895; Secretary '95, '96; Sophomore Exhibition; Sophomore Exhibition Committee; Junior X; Class Historian.

SAMUEL DAVIS. "He stood awhile on one foot, and then awhile on t'other." Entered the L. H. S. in 1895; Board of Directors A. A. '98.

EDITH DAVIS. "A whisper woke the air." Entered the L. H. S. in 1895; Sophomore Exhibition Committee: Observer Board; Junior X Committee; Junior X.

EDITH DRESSER. "That shapely hand and slender wrist
Had facile power to form a fist."
Entered the L. H. S. in 1895.

MABEL DONOVAN. "Ah me! when shall I marry me?
Lovers are plenty but fail to relieve me."
Entered the L. H. S. in 1895; Sophomore Exhibition Committee; Sophomore Exhibition; Junior X Committee; Junior X; Sophomore and Junior Decorating Committee; Senior Reception Committee; Pin Committee; 4 Class Day Committee.

INEZ EARLE. "A dozen engagements I 've broken.
   I left in the midst of a set,
   Likewise a proposal half spoken
   That waits on the stairs for me yet."
Entered the L. H. S. in 1895; Vice President '95, '96; Observer Board.

DAISY EBERHART. "That tongue of hers will get her into trouble." Entered
   the L. H. S. in 1895.

JOHN FRASER. "Pleased with a rattle, tickled with a straw." Entered the L. H.
   S. in 1895; Captain Base Ball Team '98, '99.

EMMA FULLER. "Her mind her kingdom, her will her law." Entered the L. H.
   S. in 1895.

GERTRUDE FOSTER. "What would people say if I came to the banquet without
   my bouquet?" Entered the L. H. S. in 1894; Banquet Committee.

FLORENCE GREEN. "I 'm not as green as one might think and some day may
   n't be Green at all." Entered the L. H. S. in 1895.

CHARLES HOWARD. "O! he 's a grave man." Entered the L. H. S. in 1895;
   Banquet Committee.

HAROLD HEDGES. "Blessings on thee little man." Entered the L. H. S. in 1895;
   Finance Committee; Sophomore Exhibition Committee; Treasurer '97, '98;
   Junior X Committee; Junior X; Sophomore and Junior Decorating Com
   mittee; Observer Board; Pin Committee; Advertising Manager Oracle
   Board.

PHIL HASTY. "Stiff in opinion, always in the wrong." Entered the L. H. S. in
   1895. Sophomore Exhibition Committee; Junior X Committee; Junior
   Decorating Committee; President '98, '99; Class Day Committee.

EARL HAMILTON. "Yon Cassius hath a lean and hungry look." Entered the L.
   H. S. in 1895.

NED HOPKINS. "Thinks the earth obliged to whirl
   As he the crank may choose to twirl."
Entered the L. H. S. in 1895. Sophomore Exhibition; Chairman Junior X
Committee; President '97; Junior X; Board of Directors A. A. '98; Chair-
man Pin Committee.

MABEL HUDSON. "What sweet little hats she does wear." Entered the L. H. S.
   in 1895; Vice President '96, '97; Sophomore Exhibition; Observer Board;
   Junior X.
   C

ELSIE HOPPHAN.   "Give me a look,
                    Give me a face,
                    That makes simplicity a grace."
Entered the L. H. S. in 1895.

RUTH HUME.   "If she do frown 't is not in hate of you."   Entered the L. H. S. in
1895.

CLARK JAGGER.   There 's Jagger.   He 's singing and what do I hear?
                    Listen the music that falls on the ear:
                    He 's singing, they tell me, his favorite air.
                    These are the words, "There 'll be no parting there."
                    Often we think as we list to the air,
                    Think he, we wonder like us, of his hair.
                    Editor's work makes it daily more spare.
                    We 're thinking there 'll soon be "no parting there."
Entered the L. H. S. in 1895; Treasurer in '95, '96; President S. C. A. '98;
Junior X Committee; Junior X; Observer Board; Junior Decorating Com-
mittee; Senior Reception Committee; Treasurer A. A. '98, '99; Editor-in-
Chief of Oracle.

MILLIE KOONSMAN.   "O! richly fell the flaxen hair
                    Over the maiden's shoulders fair."
Entered the L. H. S. in 1895; Commencement Orator.

JESSIE LAIRD.   "Since 't was evident she would follow her own bent."   Entered
the L. H. S. in 1896; Sophomore Exhibition: Sophomore and Junior Decorating Committee; Junior X Committee; Oracle Board.

DRAKE MEADE.   "Here lies the late lamented Mr. Meade
                    Always conspicuous for want of speed."
Entered the L. H. S. in 1894.

ROY MOORE.   "As mild and patient as the gentlest child!"   Entered the L. H. S.
in 1895.   Banquet Committee.

MARY MARTIN.   "The mild expression spoke a mind
                    In duty firm, composed, resigned."
Entered the L. H. S. in 1895.

MAME McCLORY.   "Black were her eyes as the berry that grows on the thorn by
the wayside."   Entered the L. H. S. in 1895.

MILDRED MOON.   "I sometimes sit beneath the trees
                    And read my own sweet songs."
Entered the L. H. S. in 1895; Observer Board; Class Poet.

LULU NEWLON. Devoted, anxious, generous, void of guile,
And with her whole heart's welcome in her smile.
Entered the L. H. S. in 1895.

MARIE NICHOLS. "Her looks composed and steady eye
Bespoke a matchless constancy."
Entered the L. H. S. in 1895.

CLARA OSBAND. "None knew her but to love her,
Nor named her but to praise."
Entered the L. H. S. in 1895.

JAMES PORTER. "Wise from the top of his head up." Entered the L. H. S. in
1894; Base Ball Manager '99; Junior X; Class Day Committee.

LILLIAN POWERS. "Airy, fairy Lillian!
Flitting, fairy Lillian."
Entered the L. H. S. in 1895.

BEULAH PRATT. "In her chin is a delicate dimple
By Cupid's own fingers impressed."
Entered the L. H. S. in 1895; Junior X.

ARTHUR REASONER. "Yet verily is that man a marvel." Entered the L. H. S. in
1895; Color Committee; President '97, '98; Junior X; Senior Reception Committee; Oracle Board; Commencement Orator.

HELEN ROBSON. "The rising blushes that her cheeks o'er spread
Are opening roses in the lilies' bed."
Entered the L. H. S. in 1895; Secretary '98, '99; Junior X.

LILLIAN RENNER. "There was one, the singer of our crew." Entered the L. H.
S. in 1895; Junior X; Art Editor of Oracle.

LULA ROBERTSON. "So wise, so young,
They say do ne'er live long."
Entered the L. H. S. in 1895.

MARIAN SEELEY. "Alas! I shall despair, there is no creature loves me." Entered the L. H. S. in 1895; Secretary '96, '97; Sophomore Decorating Committee; Junior X Committee; Assistant Editor Oracle; Banquet Committee.

ISABEL SIDEBOTHAM. "I know her by the quiet faithfulness with which she does
her duty." Entered the L. H. S. in 1897.

EFFIE SMITH. "Quiet, unruffled, always just the same
Like some sweet picture from a picture frame."
Entered the L. H. S. in 1895.

ARTHUR TRACY. "Have you seen our baby, Little Tot?" Entered the L. H. S. in 1895.

ALICE TOOLAN. "Her voice was ever soft, gentle, and low." Entered the L. H. S. in 1895.

LAVINA TOBIN. "I hate a match." Entered the L. H. S. in 1895; Observer Board.

JULIA VAN BUREN. "If she will, she will you may depend on 't.
If she wont, she wont; so there 's an end on 't."
Entered the L. H. S. in 1895.

THEO. WARDWELL. "I am as constant as the northern star." Entered the L. H. S. in 1895.

MARGARET YOUNG. "She wept and bewailed that she had nothing to live for." Entered the L. H. S. in 1897.

FLOYD WILSON. "Oh! as the bee upon the flower, I hang
Upon the honey of thy eloquent tongue."
Entered the L. H. S. in 1895.

JOHN WIMBLE. "Half bold, half timid, yet lazy all through." Entered the L. H. S. in 1895; Observer Board.

THE SENIOR CLASS.

Seniors

CLASS OFFICERS

President, PHILIP HASTY.
Vice President, OLIVE BRISBIN.
Secretary, HELEN ROBSON.
Treasurer, AUSTIN BRANT.

Colors: Crimson and Gold.

CLASS YELL

Euenekonta Ennea!
Right in line!
Lansing High School!
Ninety-nine!

Motto: "To reap the harvest you must sow the seed."

SENIOR CLASS OFFICERS.
AUSTIN BRANT   OLIVE BRISBIN
HELEN ROBSON   PHILIP HASTY

Juniors

Grace Allen
Amy Buckirk
Julius Baumgras
Donald Bates
Clough Burnett
Beulah Broas
Caddie Brucker
Bon Bennett
Florence Birdsall
Mabel Briggs
Nellie Blair
Grace Boyer
Fannie Bangs
Laura Butterfield
Gussie Cole
Milton Caine
Lois Cowles
Eva Cooley
Grace Cooper
Helen Canfield
Edna Clarke
Metta Cook
Daisy Chapin
Julia Curtiss
Lyle Demorest
Otis Dane
Helen Decker
Kathryn Dix
Lora Dunker
Andres Eichele
John Flanagan
Albert Fraser
Maud Goodenow
Myra Gates
Leela Goodrich
Marshall Graham
Ralph Goodenow
Arthur Green
Clara Hornberger
Eva Hill
Mary Havens
Dora Higgins
Matie Hunelberger
Katherine Hopkins
Cameron Hartness

Will Hill
Claude Hornberger
Agnes Jones
Linna Kennedy
Med Lauzen
Otto Lyon
Anabel Lang
Celia Loranz
Kate Larned
Edith Longstreet
Margret Lesy
Alma Lockhart
Mary McCornick
Gertrude Madden
Dell Moon
Harald McKale
Ray North
Emma Nottingham
Mabelle Northrop
Katherine Ostrander
Marie Piatt
Bertha Pallock
Carrie Palmer
Ray Ramage
Mary Roach
Mabel Smith
Mary Safford
Mabel Smiley
Addie Shaw
Lisle Smith
Ross Sanderson
Mabel Tubbs
Amanda Tornblom
Frank Tufts
Merle Urquhart
Nettie Van Wagoner
Fred Van Gorder
Bell Waldo
Sadie Welcher
Blanche Watson
Mabel Wood
Harry Wilson
Ralph Wheeler
Harry Ward
Mabel Yakely

Lorenzo Zimmer

Juniors

CLASS OFFICERS

President, MILTON CAINE.
Vice President, NETTIE VAN WAGONER.
Secretary, KATE LARNED.
Treasurer, MED LAUZEN.

REPRESENTATIVES ON THE ORACLE BOARD

Ray North
Nettie Van Wagoner

Colors: Yellow and White

CLASS YELL

Haikawashi Hukawashi
Haikawashi Boo!
1900! 1900!
Hip! Rah! Zoo!

Motto: "What is worth doing at all is worth doing well."

JUNIOR X COMMITTEE

Ray North, Chairman
Clough Burnett
Cameron Hartness
Merle Urquhart
John Flannagan

Florence Birdsall
Clara Hornberger
Mable Strang
Bon Bennett
Katherine Dix
Mabelle Chapin

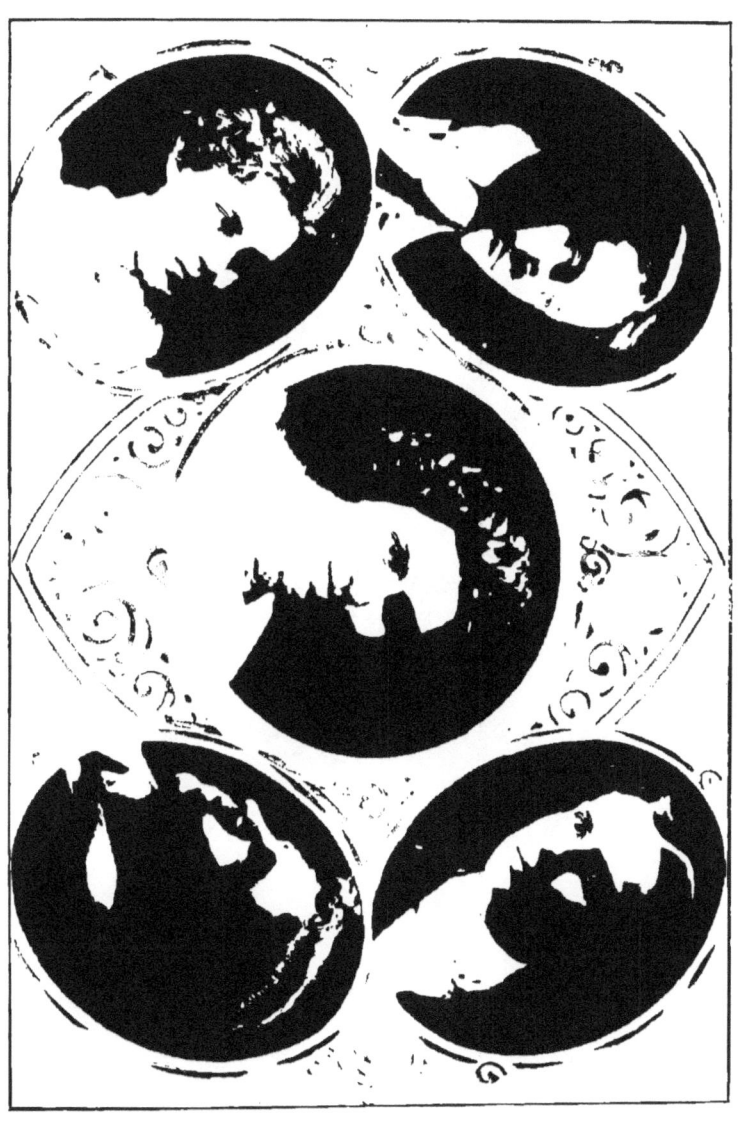

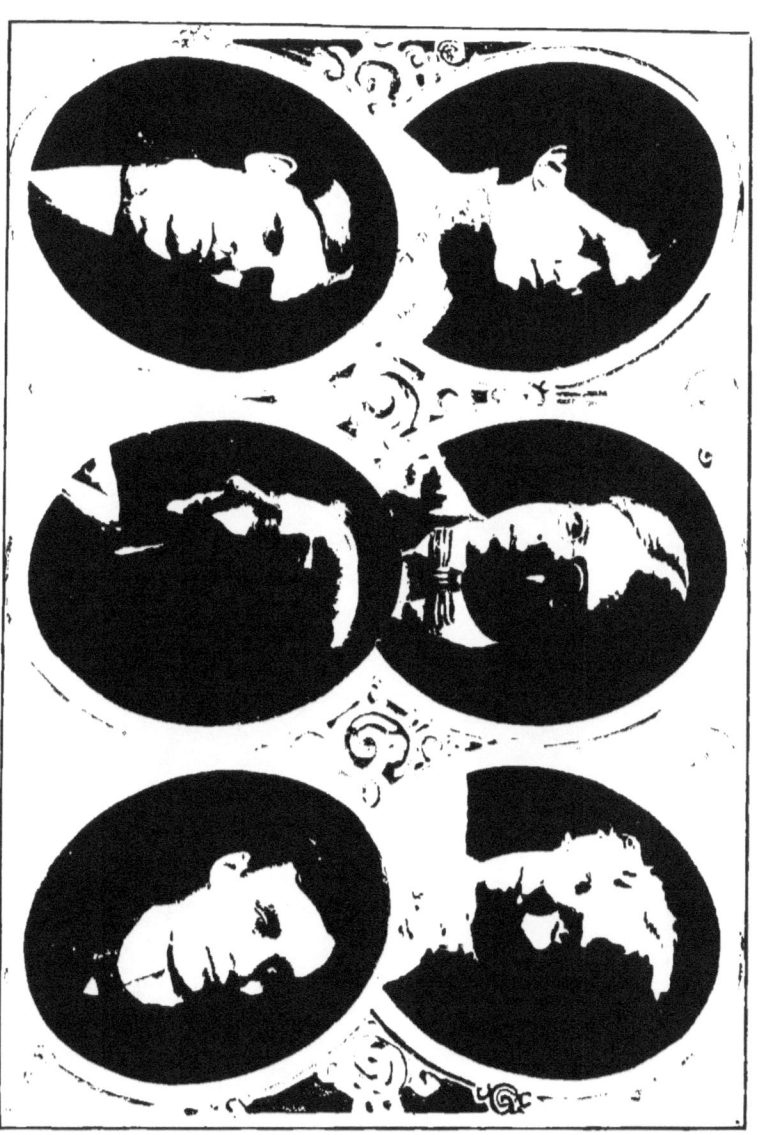

SOPHOMORE CLASS OFFICERS.

Sophomores

Hazel Atchinson
Margaret Acker
Amy Barringer
Lena Baumgras
Harrie Backus
Helen Baker
Linna Bassett
Morton Barrows
Robert Ballord
Henry B. Baker, Jr.
Burton Baker
Asa Beverly
Charlotta Brant
Josie Brodhagen
Mae Butterfield
Arthur Campbell
Robert Campbell
Clara Campbell
Tena Clear
Harold Childs
Bertha Chase
Mertie Christopher
Charles Clippert
Laura Cameron
Ethel Conner
Irene Cooper
King Casner
Maud Castner
Frank Dains
Florence Day

George Hopkins
Harriet Horning
Florence Hunter
Roger Humphrey
Lois Hull
Tella Hulburt
Callie Isbell
Henry W. Jones
Gertrude Kettle
Claribel Kennedy
Ottie Kroonsman
Merton Kirk
Riley Lyon
Ellis Laselle
Pansy Loomis
Martha Lamphere
Grace Lippincott
Mildred Mathews
Edward Miner
Robert Maier
Ford McCarrick
Marion Maltby
Tracy McCallum
Pearl Newman
Eirene Osborne
Rex Plummer
Fannye Parmlee
Ethel Plowman
Howard Piatt
Farry Parke

Anna Dermont
Fred Dillingham
Atha De Con
Estelle De Camp
Willie Dickson
Roy Dillingham
Roy Eberhart
Anna Erb
Pearl Eisman
Anna Ewing
Belle Farrand
Carrie Frey
Blanche Freedman
Margaret Forester
Lillian Frost
Victor Gardner
Molissa Goodwin
Grant Graham
Aron Gregor
Earl Gunn
Ruth Gunnison
Francis Hart
Mildred Harpster
Eugene Hammond
Alice Hewit
Mary Helmer

Harry Purvis
Drury Porter
Henry Roach
Harry Switzer
Jessie Sutherland
Margret Shattuck
Isola Smith
Mamie Smith
Pearl Smith
Bessie Stevens
Walter Shuttleworth
Henry Schneider
Barley Thoman
Lane Thorne
Bessie Twaik
Bessie Taylor
Katherine Frierweller
Jonette Templeton
Mait Wheeler
Charles Woodbury
Bertha Wait
Celia Wynegar
Grace Whiteley
Irene Wilcox
Dottie Wilson
Fanny Wood

The Sophomore Class

Who, on entering the High School assembly room, would recognize the sedate Sophomores of this year, as being the meek and timid Freshmen of last year, but such they are, although altered, *perhaps* for the better, in a great many respects.

They deemed it their special privilege, when another flight of stairs was added to their daily labors, to raise their heads a little higher and entertain more lofty views of the surroundings.

As, by their indescribable actions this year, they seem to have forgotten the fact that it was only last year that they themselves bore the cherished name of Freshmen, likewise next year, judging from their predecessors, they will probably be regardless that they ever bore the name of Sophomores.

Perhaps it is a puzzle to some to account for the disappearance of certain names on the Sophomore enrollment list of this year that appeared in the Freshmen list of last year. Of course some, after completing their Freshman year, felt capable of entering upon Life's duties without further instructions, but may be at some time you may meet one of these missing names in the hall or on the stairs, and if you are led on by your desire to solve the puzzle as to where their destination is, will at last lose sight of your object and find yourself confronted by a door, on which is the notice "Miss Lott's Room."

"Rest, rest to the weary."

With what pitying glances of compassion do the domineering Seniors regard us, as they file into the assembly room to recite their Arithmetic, of which this is an example: "If Johnnie had ten marbles, and sold half of them to Willie, how many had he remaining?"

We all feel that we are an extraordinary brilliant class, and are confident that after the year 1901 there will be a great many improvements in the world.

CLARIBEL KENNEDY.

There's one chair that is vacant,
  There's one voice missed in song,
When Mr. Holmes leads chapel
  Down with the Freshman throng.

Said he, "What lovely hair you have--
  Massed gold beneath your hats."
She turned her head to hide her face
  And softly whispered "Rats!"

Lives there a boy with soul so dead,
Who never to himself hath said,
As on his bed shone morning light,
"I wisht the school burnt down last night."

THE FATE OF THE L. H. S.

'00
The Juniors, they are naughty;
'02
The Freshmen, naughty, too;
'01
The Sophomores are naughty ones;
Pray what are we coming to?

What is it bids us bide at home,
Forbids us any more to roam,
But stay at home and make our moan?
        La Grippe.

What is it brings us teachers new?
What is it makes things run askew?
What is it gives us naught to do?
        La Grippe.
                    —M. M. M.

PRIMER

THE
FRESHMAN

D

Freshmen

CLASS OFFICERS

President, John Harden
Vice President, Edith Kositchek
Secretary, Mabel Wood
Treasurer, Fred Dean

REPRESENTATIVES ON ORACLE BOARD

Earl Jarrard
Carrie Warren

Colors: Blue and Brown

CLASS YELL

?

Motto: " We can because we think we can."

FRESHMEN CLASS OFFICERS.

EARL JARRARD
MABEL WOOD
JOHN HARDEN
EDITH KOSITCHEK
FRED DEAN
CARRIE WARREN

Freshmen.

Sula Ackerman
Bertha Abbot
Marjorie Austin
Lena Bunell
Ethel Baker
Marguerete Barrows
Sadie Barnes
Clara Ball
Merle Bradish
Bert Bryce
Erma Brown
Stella Bailey
Eva Blum
Bert Butterfield
Rhoda Boyce
Arthur Brice
Frank Brisbin
Albert Baier
Harry Brisbin
Frida Bonner
Verna Beverly
Myrtle Buck
Harold Brown
Florence Beck
Gordon Beasley
Orland Barnes
Maude Curtis
Arthur Cook
Silas Champe
John Chapman
Ada Conn
Alice Cowles
Josie Christrancy

Elenrie Cleinner
Bertha Carpenter
Mary Clippert
Frank Capin
Mable Clapham
Gertrude Coleman
Ward Clement
Leo Cahill
Clara Cailey
Glenn Canyne
Don Childs
Inez Cook
Jay Clark
Kira Curtis
Harry Curry
Grace Dresser
Laura Donovan
Frank Dodge
Lacorda Davidson
George Day
Fred De Camp
Mollie Drum
Fred Dorsey
Eddie Dunnebacke
Fred Dean
Paul Ellis
Lydia Edwards
Charles French
Leroy Fulton
George Flowers
Will Gordon
Julia Grant
Fritz Graissle

who had charge of the keys and had gone to visit a friend, appeared and unlocked the doors."

"What a good boy!"

"A few of the Juniors kindly came to receive the Freshmen, and to make up for the absence of their companions, sent for some teachers to come down post haste and give them an object lesson in acting as hosts."

"Wonderful that such wise gentlemen and ladies should require assistance."

"When it was nearly time to leave, all the arrangements for the reception were completed."

"So the Juniors know a little something about entertaining?"

"Yes, and of course the Freshmen were glad of an opportunity to thank them for their cordial welcome, condescending attentions, and charming hospitality."

To the Juniors, respectfully (?) submitted,

FRESHIE.

Flowering Currant

The clatter of children's shoes and the rattle of lunch pails echoed in the hall, and then the children scampered away down the steps and across the fresh, cool grass, half wild to escape into the May sunshine.

The teacher stood in the door-way and smiled to see their eagerness. "Good-night, teacher!" came back the chorus, and she smiled and nodded to them. Laughing, and playing pranks on one another, too full of pent-up energy to be still one moment, they raced down the hill and disappeared around the bend of the road. Long after they had gone from sight she could hear their merry voices, and the gleeful laughter came back like the tinkle of silver bells at twilight.

The shadows had begun to reach out long, dark fingers towards the east and the air grew cooler. Helen Frost turned away from the door-way and went into the school room. She seated herself at her desk and began to turn over a pile of test papers which lay there, but somehow she could not feel at all in sympathy with the work. Bones and muscles, functions and diseases, mixed themselves in a confused mass in her brain, and at last she let the paper drop on the table. "I can't work," she thought, "and I ought not to dream away the time, but somehow I can't help it, I'm so tired."

She looked about the school room which had been occupied by little ones full of life and energy, who had busied her all day long. It required all her patience and tact to keep the busy brains employed and the restless bodies from getting tired of quiet. They had come to think that "Miss Frost knew 'most everything," and from the least to the greatest they admired and loved her.

Many things did the little teacher teach them which were not in the text-books, going with them on long rambles in the woods, and teaching them in her own sweet, quiet way the things which made them think; the things which made them touch lovingly the frail wild flowers and often made the wildest, roughest boy in school drop the stone he intended to "shy" at the robin on the fence, even when he was alone.

"I don't know why," he confided to his chum, "but I just can't do it, after what she said about birds one morning, and talking as if she loved every pin-feather on 'em; and wild flowers—I can't step on 'em after her asking us if we ever thought what a great Artist it must be who could make so many kinds and colors and put 'em in such wonderful shapes. When she told us about some plants and how they grow she made it seem as if they were half like folks."

All day Helen had been busy, and now they were gone, the school room was still, and she was so tired.

The sun sank lower and lower and the last beams slanted in at the west window until they touched her face. They played hide and seek in her hair, lighting up the brown waves until they looked like gold. At last the sun sank down behind the low fringe of trees in the distance.

She rose and went to the open window, and kneeling down with one hand on the sill and the other under her cheek, she looked out at the sunset, which grew radiantly beautiful each moment.

Just beneath the window grew a great flowering-currant bush. Every year the eager children gathered their hands full of the blossoms, and the bees ravaged it of honey, but it flourished on in unabated vigor. The top-most branches swayed in the light wind and brushed the cheek of the young girl kneeling at the window. She broke a spray from the bush, her slender fingers touching the blossoms tenderly, almost reverently.

The spicy fragrance made her almost faint. She was no longer in the little school room. She sat by the western window of a large studio looking out across the green fields and silvery waters of the river, watching just such a sunset as this behind the green hills of the Hudson. Shadows were beginning to nestle in the hollows on the eastern side of the slopes, but the tops were crowned with rose and yellow light and the west was crimson.

She had been trying for a week to catch the wonderful light of the sunset on the river and the light and shade of the hills in the approaching twilight, but somehow the result of her labor, though beautiful, failed to satisfy her exacting, æsthetic soul.

Tonight, it seemed to her, the sunset was more beautiful than it had ever been before. She had dropped her brushes involuntarily and was leaning forward lost in admiration.

Jack, the studio boy, who ran errands, cleaned brushes and scrubbed up paint stains, making his small self generally useful, came and picked up her brushes and palette unheeded.

The shadows began to chase each other farther and farther up the slopes and still she lingered, charmed by the quiet beauty of the scene before her. The students had gone long ago.

The artist had been sitting by a southern window looking over some sketches. He rose quietly and came and stood beside her, looking at the painting unfinished on her easel. "What is it, Helen ; can you not finish it? You have done well." She started, and looked up at him with eyes bright with emotion and exclaimed, "It's too beautiful—I can't do it, and yet I so long to!"

"Our best is always beyond us," he answered softly.

With a quick, caressing movement he laid his hand upon her head, where it rested only a moment, then dropped to his side. She looked up at him wonderingly, and the brown eyes looked down into the clear blue ones. Then the blood rushed into her cheeks and the long lashes drooped. She rose quickly, and in so doing put out her hand towards the statue of Venus which stood beside her, but the artist's hand intercepted hers in its journey and held it fast.

She would not look at him, although he waited for her to do so, and at length he said, "Helen, I am such a strange, silent man that I fear I shall shock and frighten you by what I want to say to you." He hesitated, and then said, "Do you care for me at all—more than you do for other men?"

She did not answer at once, and when she did look at him it was with a puzzled expression in her eyes as she said, "Why do you ask me such a question, Mr. Ashley?"

"I know it surprises you ; it is a strange way for me to put it, but what I say to you now I must say in my own way. Can you trust me enough to answer it just as I asked it?"

Her eyes met his steadily now, and she answered in a low voice, "Yes, I do."

"God bless you for that, Helen; some day I shall want to tell you something else, but I must not now—for my mother's sake." Then before she realized it, he was gone.

As Helen walked home in the beautiful twilight she was puzzled and surprised. How strange the events of the last half hour seemed as she thought of them now. She felt as if she had been dreaming.

"'For his mother's sake,'" she thought; "I wonder what he meant. I wonder who it was who said

"God be thanked, the meanest of his creatures
Boasts two soul sides, one to face the world with,
One to show a woman when he loves her."

Helen had no memory of her father; he had died when she was a tiny child, but the sweet mother who died five years later she remembered and longed for. She had lived with an old aunt, until when Helen was eighteen, she too had died. Her mother had one brother, Joe, the wild boy who had run away to sea and never returned. How she wished she knew where he was, for she felt so alone. Wishing to finish her art course, she went to Mrs. West, who lived near her aunt's home, to ask if she might board there, and that lady had replied, "Why, of course you may come, Helen. I couldn't have any one else, but it seems as if you belonged to me."

As Helen reached her boarding place little Marian West bounded into her arms and deposited a dainty little missive triumphantly in her hands.

"Oh, I'm so glad you've come!" she cried. "I wondered and wondered what you were doing. The biscuits are getting so cold. Is it that tiresome picture again?"

"Yes, dear, the picture, but not tiresome."

She stood at the gate and opened the note, Marian meanwhile watching her impatiently. No one was allowed to touch Helen's letters except herself, but just now the biscuits interested her more. "Hurry, Helen, hurry! What is it about?"

"Mrs. Ashley invites me to an art entertainment at her home this evening. How lovely of her!"

"And you'll wear your white dress, and my lilies-of-the-valley in your hair, and be so pretty, won't you?"

"You witch!" exclaimed Helen, but the little one sprang away and ran up the walk, closely followed by her laughing friend. Both were out of breath with the run and burst into the house with considerable noise.

"Mercy!" exclaimed Mrs. West. "What are my children doing now?"

"Marian has been making absurd remarks," said Helen.

"Children tell—" began Mrs. West.

"Not always," interrupted Helen.

"Well, tea is ready; compose yourselves if you can and make a proper appearance."

Supper over, Helen went to make her toilette. It was simple—a white gown with white ribbons, and lilies-of-the-valley in her hair and belt, but the effect was certainly a very pleasing picture, and Hugh Ashley thought so as she entered the room.

Helen had always felt a little afraid of the stately Mrs. Ashley, and to-night that lady looked more than usually queenly. She put Helen quite at her ease in a few moments, however, and the girl enjoyed the evening very much. She was in her element.

Later in the evening Mrs. Ashley came to her as she was admiring some water colors and said, "Do you care to see my latest pets, Miss Frost?" Then at Helen's puzzled look she said, "Roses."

"Indeed I do! I love flowers," said Helen.

Her hostess led the way down a long hall, out into a little conservatory on the south side of the house. She turned on the lights and said, "Here they are; aren't they beauties?" They were, indeed, and Helen wandered from one bush to another, drinking in the delicate, delicious perfume.

"You are a sensible young lady, Miss Frost, and I have something to say to you," said Mrs. Ashley at last. "I do not wish to hurt your feelings and I think you will see and understand the matter as I do. I scarcely think you see it, and I am sure he does not, but Hugh is growing to admire you too much. You are pretty and talented, child, but you are so much younger than he. I have petted his artistic longings, and indulged his fancy for teaching painting. Now he must please me and marry someone befitting his station. I know you could have no such idea as Hugh's caring for you, and that unconsciously much might be done. You are too sensible to allow such a condition of affairs to come about. I say this to put you on your guard." She said this very gracefully, unable to appreciate how each word was wounding the girl beside her.

Helen trembled. She felt too weak, almost, to stand; but her pride helped her, and though she could scarcely speak she said, "Certainly not, Mrs. Ashley." She turned back to the roses and there was a long silence.

"I knew you would not," said Mrs. Ashley, breaking the pause which was growing oppressive. "Shall we go back to the studio?"

As they passed down the long hall Helen's thoughts were busy. She must not see Hugh just now; she must have time to think.

"I think I will go out on the porch for a little while," she said "The warm air of the rooms has given me a headache. The people, will not miss me."

"Do so, my dear; perhaps the cool air will drive it away," and Mrs. Ashley threw a fleecy, white shawl over Helen's head and shoulders. She opened a side door and said, "Here is a side porch; no one will annoy you."

How cool the air felt on her face and how still the moonlight was! Flowering-currant blossoms filled the air with sweetness and the long, yellow branches hung in luxuriant profusion over the porch railing.

At first she could hardly think. She felt intensely bitter towards Mrs. Ashley, but gradually the quiet of the evening stole over her.

"She does not know," she thought. She has great ambitions for Hugh, and no wonder she cannot endure the thought of his caring for me. She didn't add that I am poor and he heir to the Ashley thousands and estate, but she might as well." Then with a sudden revulsion of feeling, "Why does she feel so? If tonight were last night I could bear it better. I must go home—he will see that something is wrong and ask what it is."

She went back into the hall and saw Mrs. Ashley standing near the door of the studio She went to her and said in a low tone, "I am going home. My headache does not grow better, and I will go quietly without disturbing anyone."

"I am sorry, but if you feel that you must go I will not urge you, for I appreciate what a headache is, and you are very pale."

She went with Helen to get her hat and light shawl and accompanied her to the door.

When Helen reached home she retired as soon as possible, but she could not sleep. Her heart throbbed unmercifully and she tossed restlessly. At last she did sleep, but when she awoke in the morning her head ached harder. She tried to rise but grew faint with pain, and realized that the headache had become neuralgia. She remained in bed and felt dimly conscious that she was glad of an excuse for not going to the studio.

Towards night, thanks to Mrs. West's skilful treatment, she felt better, but too weak to go down stairs.

Hugh called to ask for her, and Mrs. West answered that she was better but still felt weak from the great pain.

"The postman brought you a letter, Helen," said Marian, when she was at last allowed to go to Helen's room. The writing was unfamiliar and Helen opened it wonderingly. She looked to see who was the writer, and the name "Aunt Carrie" puzzled her still more. She began to read and found to her great surprise that it was from Uncle Joe's wife. It was a long story of how all the years after he had come back from sea Joseph Bancroft had searched for his sister, and only now he had found her child.

Mrs. Bancroft begged Helen to visit them, and said in conclusion, "I cannot take 'no' for an answer. You must come. We are so lonely since your cousin Grace was married. I have been ill, and now that I am growing better I need you to cheer me. We both want you."

Helen's mind was made up quickly. Here was her way out. She heard Mrs. West in the room adjoining, and, calling her, she said: "I've found mother's brother, Uncle Joe, or rather, he has found me. He lives in Indiana, and Aunt Carrie has written to me. She is ill and lonely and wishes me to visit them. The idea has taken my fancy, and I think I will go to-morrow. I know it is a sudden determination, but I like to do things suddenly."

The next evening Helen was on board the train, speeding away towards the sunset. She had left a prettily worded note for Hugh, telling him how much she had enjoyed her work under his teaching, and that her departure was so sudden that she had no time to see him.

Hugh crushed it in his hand when he had read it and then smoothed it out carefully and put it in his pocket. He called at Mrs. West's that evening and carried some paint-tubes and sketches that Helen had left. He inquired where she had gone, but Mrs West suddenly remembered that Helen had only said "Indiana," and in the hurry she had forgotten to ask the name of the place.

He went home disturbed. How was he ever to find her—to learn why she went away? For he felt certain that something lay beneath that quiet, graceful little note.

As Helen watched the flying landscape from the car window she said to herself: "I shan't die; Shakespeare said men didn't, and women

don't often in real life. No, I shall live and this will not spoil my life.
I can never forget, but I can keep from growing morose and
reminding people of an animated corpse. He said our best was always
beyond us. I feel as if mine is behind me. Well, the sun's going
down—but in the morning it will rise again and it's only dark between.
There's something for me in life, and I'm going to do it, and do it well."

"You didn't stipulate when I was to come," she said laughingly,
when the first surprise of her early coming had subsided.

"You're like me, you ran away without notice," said Uncle Joe,
"But we're not going to let you be as sorry as I was," he added growing grave.

Mrs. Bancroft was quite weak after her illness, but she declared
Helen was as good as a tonic, and as autumn came she grew stronger.

As her aunt needed less and less of her attention Helen began to long
for occupation. She did not feel like painting and she began to grow
restless. Her aunt found nothing amiss in her; she was always sweet
and gentle and thoughtful; she laughed merrily and sang at her work.
No one knew it, but sometimes the blue eyes grew dark with pain.

The school district wanted a teacher, and one evening she astonished
her uncle by exclaiming: "Uncle Joe, do you think they would let me
teach the school this winter?"

"You, chick? What! do you think you could manage a school? I
warn you some of them are hard to keep in order."

"I can manage you; I'd like to try," she answered mischievously,
"I find myself like Alexander, longing for more worlds to conquer."

"Enough said," replied her uncle, laughing at his own discomfiture,
"If you are really in earnest I'll speak to the school board."

"I certainly am," she returned, and so it came about that she was
duly installed in the little school-house.

"I can do this for a while," she thought. "Then I must think of
other work in earnest."

To-night as she knelt at the window it all came back to her with the
scent of the flowering-currant.

It grew darker, the crimson clouds changed to ashen grey, and still
she knelt there motionless. She did not hear a step beside her, and
then someone said: "Helen, my dear little girl!"

"Why!" she exclaimed, too surprised for anything else.

"You ran away: did you want to go?"

It was all so sudden that she did not think, and the "no" came from
her lips involuntarily.

"Then I'm glad I found you. I've looked a long time, and at last found you through an old friend who lives here and accidentally spoke of the new teacher. I came all the way from New York to see you, and he introduced me to your uncle, or I don't suppose he would have allowed me to come in. He looked suspicious as it was'"

"But your mother?" faltered Helen.

"Mother died last fall," he answered softly, "and in her diary I found this—" producing a folded paper—'May 17. Helen Frost has gone to Indiana I wonder if she really cared, after all. Well, it is better so.' I knew then why you went away. Mother was very ambitious for me. Doctor Kadie said I must be careful that she was not greatly excited, since any intense excitement would menace her life, since she was not strong. So I tried to guard her and humor her fancies. She wished me to marry a wealthy lady, but I kept telling her that I was not ready to marry, and she seemed half pacified though not satisfied. I can say to you now what I longed to say a year ago. I love you; do you care for me still?"

"Yes—you know."

It was dark now, but the new moon's crescent glowed softly.

"You have suffered, Helen; so have I. Kiss me, dear; it is over now."

The sweet scent of the dew-wet blossoms floated in at the open window, but the odor did not pain her now. The moonlight fell on her beautiful hair, and as Hugh fastened a spray of the blossoms in its coils he said: "I told you our best was always beyond us. I feel as if it were very near me to-night."

M. MILDRED MOON.

....Organizations....

Alpha Omega Fraternity,

Chapters

Alpha, - - - - Detroit, Mich., - - Established 1897
Beta, - - - - Lansing, Mich., - Established 1898
Gamma, - - - - Sioux City, Iowa, - - Established 1899
Colors: Black and White.

Fratres in Alumnis

Clarence W. Christopher, '98   Claud E. Chamberlain, '98
Harry B. Hustan, '98

Fratres in Schola

1899
Clark B. Jagger   Arthur T. Reasoner

1900
Merle A. Urquhart   Milton A. Caine
J. Cameron Hartness   Clough T. Burnett

1901
Drury L. Porter   Eugene T. Hammond

1902
Fred M. Dean

Fratres ex Schola
Ray V. Young, '00

L. R. T.

Organized March 3, 1899

Members

Stella Bailey
Eirene Osborne

Beulah Broas
Carlotta Brant

Laura Donovan
Florence Day

Eva Shank
Hattie Whitehead
Clara Campbell

Bell Farrand
Anna Ewing

Blanche Freedman
Carrie Warren

The Jolly Owls

Though not, strictly speaking, a High School organization, yet we feel connected with that institution because if we had not been brought together there we would never have had the club. We did not intend to organize a society, but merely to make arrangements whereby a few of us might meet, after the arduous duties of the week of school work, and refresh ourselves. However, we gradually grew into a sort of semi-organization and drew up a constitution. Many a heart has been made lighter and many a brain cleared by these little oases along the desert life of school. The following is our membership:

Mable Briggs
  Florence Birdsall
    Clough Burnett
      Eva Cooley
        Milton Caine
Irene Cooper
  Grace Cooper
    Cameron Hartness
      Clark Jagger

Marie Piatt
  Howard Piatt
    Harry Purvis
      Drury Porter
        Margaret Sipley
Ross Sanderson
  Lisle Smith
    Merle Urquhart
      Mabel Yakely

Students' Christian Association

Organized in 1886

Ross Sanderson, President
    Miss Atkins, Vice President
        Mildred Moon, Secretary
           Harold McKale, Treasurer

MEMBERS

Erma Brown	Mildred Moon
Eva Cooley	Marie Nichols
Belle Cady	Lillian Renner
Milton Caine	Arthur Reasoner
Edith Dresser	Ernestine Robinson
Grace Dresser	Maggie Rolfe
Clarence Holmes	Amy Byan
Ruth Hume	Isabella Sidebotham
Dora Higgins	Effie Smith
Clark Jagger	Guy Smith
Mildred Koonsman	Grace Smith
Emma Lott	Lisle Smith
Harold McKale	Merle Urquhart

Board of Directors

Of the Athletic Association

President, CAMERON HARTNESS
Vice President, HERBERT BARRINGER
Secretary, MED LAUZEN
Treasurer, CLARK JAGGER

Class Representatives

Senior, AUSTIN BRANT
Junior, CLOUGH BURNETT
Sophomore, DRURY PORTER
Freshman, GEORGE DAY

BOARD OF DIRECTORS, ATHLETIC ASSOCIATION.

Alumni Association

Officers

President, - - - - - - CLARENCE BEMENT, '74
Vice President. - - - - - Miss HALLA COOK, '96
Secretary, - - - - - - H. MERTON CLARK, '98
Treasurer. - - - - - - - FRANK McKIBBIN, '97

Board of Directors

GRACE HAGADORN, '94   CLINTON WARD, '95   BERTHA WEMPLE, '96
CLARA GOWER, '97   WM. HUMPHREY, '98

Education

The education which is of real value is that which makes us citizens of the world, men and women who can respond with sympathy and success to all the varied pulsations of Life in highly civilized nations. In all probability one could find no better test of a person's education than his ability to read, and to read understandingly and with interest, the various articles in our best periodicals. To absorb and comprehend the happenings of the whole wide world as one comes to know of them may well be made that for which we are striving educationally. So far as understanding and appreciating the progress which the world is making is concerned, we may well consider it a supreme test for our individual educational attainment, and the ways and means by which we have accomplished all this may be said to comprise a test of the utility of the various branches of study and methods of instruction.

Thus we go on each year, keeping what we believe to be of value and what has been an aid, and casting out that which seems superfluous.

Dr. Schuman, in the *School Review*, Feb., 1894, insists that education is not merely a training of the mental powers; it is a process of nutrition; mind grows by what it feeds upon. And the mental organism, like the physical, must have suitable and appropriate nourishment Now, if the school can put the pupil in harmony with the spirit of intelligence, can endow him with the thought habit, and can make him understand the necessity for using, and teach him to use the tools of acquirement and expression, we may trust the rest with every prospect of success to the after-school period of his life.

With this prospect in view, the amount of English required in all of the courses in the school has been increased, and English is coming to be considered one of the most important studies in the curriculum. In place of the old method of teaching English, that of talking about literature and reading very little, has come an earnest desire to know something about our authors and their writings, and the plan of editing the classics has placed within easy reach of the pupil much valuable reading material. The following from William Dean Howells covers that ground completely and contains a kernel of wisdom:

"For my own part, I believe I have never got any good from a book that I did not read merely because I wanted to read it. I think this may be applied to any thing a person does. The book, I know, which you read from a sense of duty, or because for any reason you must, is apt to yield you little. This, I think is also true of every thing, and the endeavor that does one good — and lasting good — is the endeavor one makes with pleasure."

We may labor in an entirely different spirit and something may be accomplished, but that which we do cheerfully and with pleasure is sure to bring the greatest reward.

An English philosopher is authority for the saying that "reading maketh a full man." We know also that too much reading without careful selection is also liable to make a dull man; and the brain, as well as the stomach, may be overfed and with parallel results.

I think I am safe in saying that one excellent way to continue our education after leaving the High School is by reading, and the abundance of periodicals and books published in these days furnishes us with material that is both cheap and wholesome from which to select, and while nothing more unfortunate can happen to the intellectually growing person than to be possessed of the novel reading habit, there is no doubt that a good, cheerful novel, respectably written, may be made to form a very profitable diversion from the more fatiguing efforts of study or work.

It follows, then, that in no way can the object sought in the education of the young be better attained than by providing them with good, wholesome and attractive literature, and thus it becomes the duty of Boards of Education to provide such literature, suitable and accessible to pupils of all ages. Thus one of the greatest helps in the process of education will be established by assisting the child to broaden and develop that power, the germ of which he already posesses; for education means the creation of nothing new, but rather the unfolding and developing of that faculty which our Divine Father hath implanted within us.

CLARENCE E. HOLMES.

President's Address

To the friends gathered here, to the teachers who have been our guides, and to our fellow students and class-mates, it is my privilege to give a last greeting. The occasion is both sad and glad. I will not at this time bring "the eternal note of sadness" in, but speak rather of the brighter, better part, which is strong and enduring and full of hope.

There are those present tonight who hold especial claims upon our gratitude:—our superintendent, whose strong, earnest words and faithful example must ever be, as they have been, an inspiration to us; teachers, whose patience we have so often tried and whose best-laid plans ofttimes have been thwarted by our heedlessness. We thank you all for the sacrifices you have made for us; we can not repay you, but we know that our lives will be the better and stronger for the good influences with which you have surrounded us. To many of us the education we have obtained here will be our only capital in beginning life, and whatever measure of success we may hereafter attain we shall owe largely to our school and our teachers. In the name of the class, I would express the wish that your memory of us may be as pleasant as ours will always be of you.

It is well to "welcome the coming, speed the parting guest." As we finish our High School life, our places are quickly to be filled by others. We welcome you, our fellow students of the Class of 1900. To you we yield our places. The duties and privileges which were once ours will largely become yours. It will be your duty to attend Chapel exercises and Senior Orations and your privilege to take up your abode in a place less high (in air). May you perform your duties more faithfully; may you fill our places with greater credit. What need I say more than to wish you well for the time to come?

Fellow Classmates, our High School days are ended, and whether or not we are saying good bye to each other, we are saying good bye to the old school days. We shall walk the familiar halls and climb the stairs no more together. The thoughtless words, the petty ambitions and jealousies, have become things of the past; but whatever of joy or sorrow the future may have in store for us, we shall ever retain and cherish this precious possession—the memory of these happy days. Nothing can rob us of this. The little commonplaces of the school room, the quaint situations, the unexpected answers, even the peculiarities of each one, will be treasured. We have been laying the foundations on which to build our future characters. We have been taught that truthfulness is the foundation of moral excellence. Not only veracity of speech but sincerity of mind. We have been taught to admire courage and to desire it; moral courage as well as physical. We have been taught to wrong no one by thought, word or deed, shaping our actions by the lofty principles of the Golden Rule. These and many other invaluable qualities have often been presented to our view, and we should see to it that they are deeply and firmly imbedded in these foundations.

And now in parting let us remember that

" This world is full of interesting things;

We all ought to be as happy as kings,"

and subdue all feelings except those of gladness. I can wish for nothing higher or happier in the days to come than that in the brightest sunshine or the inevitable shadow, we may have the consciousness of duty faithfully performed, and that each year and each day of our lives may be marked by improvement, both intellectual and moral, and that each of us may live with the desire uppermost in the mind which is expressed by the poet in the words:

"Build thee more stately mansions, O my soul!

As the swift seasons roll!

Leave thy low-vaulted past!

Let each new temple, nobler than the last,

Shut thee from heaven with a dome more vast,

Till thou at length art free,

Leaving thine outgrown shell by life's unresting sea!"

PHILIP HASTY.

Class Poem

The Life Ship.

I stand beside the sea at even-tide
And look across the deep. The waters glide
With softest ripple up the pebbly strand.
Then sink again. The gray old ocean, spanned
By star-lit heavens, sleeps ; but sleeping, still
Moans in its slumber, tossed by dreams of ill.
Over the waters dark the moon shines down ;
The light-house beacon gleams above the town ;
The day has gone and now the vanished sun
Lights up the twinkling star-lamps, one by one.

At rest, her keel upon the shining sands,
A boat, new-built, awaits the touch of hands
To launch her. Ere three suns shall throw
Rose-lights across the east, and paint the glow
Of sunset in the west, she sails away,
Out, out--far out beyond the bay.

I think I see her as she glides away
Out from the home port at the close of day;
Each bolt, each plate, each timber, mast, and band
As strong as willing heart and skillful hand
Can make them ; while to catch the favoring gales,
Like great birds' wings are spread the snowy sails.
The sun shines brightly and the water gleams
With lights of gold and pearl. The soft wind seems

To bear sweet odors from far-off shore,
To greet the eager sailors, and the roar
Of Ocean sinks.   Day after day she sails.
The west grows rosy, and the last star pales
Before the morning's sun, and all is well.

But by and by, far o'er the Ocean's swell
Is seen a little cloud.   It strengthens fast
Until the whole blue heaven is overcast
With threat'ning clouds.   The angry waves roll high
The lightning flashes, and the thunders cry
With sullen voices to the roaring sea.
Night comes   dark night; the wind howls loud in glee.
The cold rain drives against the close-reefed sails
And mingles with the spray.   The look-out fails
To catch the faintest gleam of friendly light
To guide the good ship through the raging night.
The morn dawns, gray and cloudy; all day long
The storm growls fiercely, but the ship is strong
And rides the waves full bravely.   When the sun
Wheels towards the west and day is nearly done
The waves grow calm, the rain-drops cease, and bright
Against the sunset gleams the harbor-light.

What shall I say to you, O sailors true,
You who sailed out, far out across life's blue?
" Men should be what they seem."   Seem true, be so!
Day after day, as on through life you go,
The world will peer, a cynic, in your eyes.
Let it find them as clear as summer skies
Untouched by cloud.   Face storms with steady heart;
'Tis base to stand-aside and leave your part
Undone to make some other's burden more
Or else to lie a wreck upon life's shore.
Do it yourself.   Whatever be your place,
Make its work kingly by the royal grace

With which you do it. Think you he is less
Because with hardened hands and sooty dress,
The fireman tends the roaring fires, whose force
Speeds the good ship upon her seaward course?
Useless, without his work, the captain's skill,
Each his own place, where e'er it be, must fill.
The sailor-garb would be but idle show
Without the sailor-heart that throbs below.

Think not each craft that carries not your sign
Bears ill to you, or has some dark design.
Believe that men are true, and often you
May make them so. Better prove them untrue
Than make them so by doubt. Seek for the best
All hearts, all lands, can yield at your request.

And you who had the task to train the crew.
You have been faithful, and we owe to you
Much that we are and much we hope to be.
I know our voyage over life's great sea
Will not be all in sunshine. Clouds will rise;
Sometimes the waves will seem to meet the skies.
But by-and-by the Good Ship, weather-worn,
Storm-tossed and battered, bruised and tempest-torn,
Shall reach her Port, and there within the Bay
Drop down her anchor at the close of Day.

And now God speed you o'er the waters bright
And keep you safe from dangers, day and night;
Until through mists we see the Bar-lights shine,
God bless our crew and Good Ship, "Ninety-nine!"

                              M. MILDRED MOON.

Class History

It is needless to say that a King never attempted to organize a more obedient or a more military-appearing band of troops than was assembled in the fall of '95. We, as Freshmen, were noted for our orderly class-meetings and general modesty of behavior.

But it is truly astonishing how quickly strife and contention arise even among the very meekest. Our struggle for Sophomore officers would have done credit to the Seniors of '98, and while our excitement was aroused we accomplished two great feats: first, a class sleigh-ride, and second, a Sophomore Exhibition. For this X we claim the honor of being the first class to demonstrate our abilities to the public at large, and to the rest of the High School, while we were still in only our second year of existence. Since then the class of '99 has been noted as a charming hostess, especially at "Chafing-dish Parties" and ten-cent café lunches à la Donsereaux.

As Juniors, we were still "en mache." After Jupiter had hurled many thunder-bolts upon us, and Mars had become well acquainted with the evils and deceits of the Juniors, we selected our class officers, Observer board, etc. That this selection of our leaders was a good one was shown by the success of our Junior X, in which our timidity appeared at the same time with our faculty for getting out of scrapes. Our wisdom was also shown by another class sleigh-ride, in which the ratio of girls to boys was, as usual, 16 to 1.

As all children must grow out of their teens, we at length became Seniors, grave and dignified, once more with peaceful assemblies and martial bearing; but with Hasty strides we were nearing this eventful week of our lives which frees us from specified "lines of force." The dollars spent in midnight oil, the concerts and parties piously sacrificed to "bohning," the sharp squalls and tempests after flunks all these are little thought of now. Indeed we remember them, but only as the dark cloud through which shone the silver lining of this June, when all cares and anxieties would be ended.

With troubled minds and quivering eyelids, we have divided and sub-divided Caesar's Gaul into numberless parts and have hurled our maledictions upon the head of the wretched Cataline. We, too, like Menelaos and wide-ruling Agamemnon, have stormed Ilium's walls in rain. We have dug deep into the mysteries of square and cube root and have vainly striven to realize how much we owe to Pascal because we know that "the pressure is transmitted undiminished in all directions and acts with the same force upon equal surfaces and at right angles to the surfaces." We have spent many afternoons in the Physical Laboratory, and in our hurry to get the 18th Sheet of Experiments finished by the end of the week, we have unluckily discovered the cost of glass jars, beakers, and thermometers. It is well known that some of the experiments which were undertaken were not found upon the Laboratory sheets. For instance, an attempt was made to find the temperature of 100 g. of snow and 50 Kg. of Hedges. The result was warmer than was anticipated, whereupon the Hedges in question was presumptuous enough to try to wash the spots from the face of the Moon.

The ability of the class as individuals is marvelous. Even we ourselves are astonished at what has been accomplished by some of our fellow-sufferers. Strange inventions, wonderful displays of oratory, and new editions of Algebras, Arithmetics, and especially Grammars have appeared. One small lad during the intervals between dinner and the first afternoon class gradually developed into composer, artist, and even poet. But this last talent, although indicative of genius almost sufficient for a class poet, met its superior in her whose scholarly ideas and depth of mind were revealed in this her first poem, entitled

"TO MY GUINEA."

I have a very funny pet;
The hens he likes to fret.
He runs at them from morn 'til night
And keeps them in a fright.

I think it tires him to do so,
For he will make them go,
And then he 'll stop—my dear, 't is true
He 'll stop and say: "O whew!"

As to our faculty, we are forced to admit that they, too, are not of
the very dullest, although one member does persist in leaving her
glasses behind; while another immediately becomes very cross at such
a small thing as a flower or ribbon of yellow. One is so very extravagant as to pay $2.00 for a very small bar of toilet soap; while the
opposite extreme is seen in another, who enjoys a good dinner all the
better when she can avoid paying for it.

Despite the dreadful lack of gray matter in the brains of our instruct-
ors, and notwithstanding the extra amount of the same in the brains of
the class of '99, for some unaccountable reason we found it profitable to
remain during these last four years. Thus we now realize that we
have learned perhaps a very little in that time, though in September of
'95 we thought such a thing impossible.

If tonight any member of this graduating class should be asked,
"has it payed to keep at work, does the profit equal the loss?" I am
sure we would all answer yes. We have gained and we know it. Not
only in what knowledge me may have of Latin or Geometry, but something more. Our minds have broadened; we have a clearer understanding of mankind, and a good foundation for becoming true and intelligent American citizens, such as will always be needed so long as our
country stands. But we have worked hard for our reward, studying
energetically through many tedious days and nights. As we look back
over it now, we see many things that were unpleasant. We realize
that many times we might have been more credit to our school and to
ourselves; but tonight we forget them all and rejoice only that we can
now say, as every other graduating class has said before us, "*veni, vidi,
vici*" with especial emphasis on the *vici*.

Still in all the gladness of Commencement, there is one small strain
of sadness. We soon will separate; some to go here, others there;
some to success, others to failure; probably never all to meet again.
But no matter how widely we may be separated, or how differently we
may be situated, there will always be one bond of sympathy, one tie

that will bind us. Whatever there may have been that we might have wished otherwise at the time, it will all be lost and only with pleasure will we look back upon our High School life, and only with gladness will we say,

Ennenekonta Ennea!
Right in line!
Lansing High School!
'99!

CLARA BELLE CADY.

Class Prophecy

Along one of the principal highways of Northern England, a solitary monk ambled on a peaceful mule. As he rode, the monk's head was bowed in deep thought and the mule seemed to be taking his time, stopping now and then unnoticed by his rider. But suddenly the mule stumbled and the monk looked up to see that he had come to a break in the woods, and that on a slight eminence, not far from him, was a solitary tower. The tower was high and built of rough stones, which were overgrown with moss and lichens. Near it was a small cottage completely covered with ivy; so much so that it could hardly be recognized from a distancee.

The monk dismounted from his mule and walked toward the tower. Looking up at the high windows he saw at one of them a sweet, pensive face gazing intently down the road, and as he looked the face of an energetic woman appeared beside the other. Immediately both faces were withdrawn. The monk turned to the lodge-keeper, who now greeted him, and asked who the ladies were. "Why, Father," said the lodge-keeper Adelbert, "the young lady is Lady Marie; she sits at the window all day, and when people ask her why she does it, she says she is watching for her knight, who is coming sometime to carry her off. The other one is Mistress Dresser, her aunt and housekeeper, and she thinks Lady Marie a silly little goose to put faith in any man."

The monk turned again to look at the tower, and saw coming from a small postern gate a Sister of Charity in her gray robes. He asked the porter who it was, and was told that it was Sister Margaret, who had, in her youth, been the bosom friend of Mistress Dresser, and that she now paid her a half-hour visit once a month; "and," continued the porter, "do you see that little cottage yonder? There lives Mother Renner and her forty cats; and if you will believe it, she spends all

F

her time in teaching them not to quarrel ; and some day she will succeed, she says." The porter paused, and the monk thanked him and returned to his mule, contentedly grazing on the side of the road. He mounted and rode thoughtfully on his way. After traveling two or three hours he came abruptly upon a narrow road, which appeared to lead into a dense forest. The road was lined on both sides with huge trees. At the end of this road a castle rose to view. The castle consisted of a large and high square tower surrounded by buildings of inferior height which were encircled by an inner courtyard. Around the outside wall was a deep moat, once full of water but now dried up.

The monk rode up to the castle. He was shown by lodge-keeper Herbert into the great hall. As the monk entered this immense room he paused and looked around him. At the end near the entrance was the great fireplace, and at the other end the tables spread for the next meal. In the embrasure of the window sat Lady Donovan, master as well as mistress of this imposing pile, since the death of her husband. She was surrounded by her maids. Marian sat near her Lady trying to embroider by the fading light, but it was easily seen that her mind was not on her work, by the tender glances she cast at something concealed in her lap. All the maids knew it was a written message from her Knight, far away. In the mighty fireplace stood a little wizened old woman, stirring some herbs in a caldron over the fire. It was Mother Bell, the herb woman, who did all the doctoring for leagues around. At her right stood Emma, at an easel, trying to paint by the fire-light. Maid Mabel sat near her, playing softly on her harp, while Millie and Ruth sang to her accompaniment. In seats on either side of the fireplace sat Mistresses Armstrong and Butts, reading their Latin most industriously. Just as Lady Donovan arose to greet the monk, down the long hall came Mistress Robertson, the housekeeper, with a great bunch of keys at her side. She asked how soon her Ladyship wished to have the evening meal served, but was interrupted by the barking of dogs, the clatter of horses' hoofs, and over all, the winding of horns. All rushed to the windows in time to see a merry party of Knights and Ladies just from the chase, ride across the drawbridge, the foremost lady carrying the brush. They all dismounted and the horses were led away by the grooms, Hopkins and Frazer, while John Wimble looked after the dogs. The merry company tripped into the great hall. First came Sir James with the lady of his choice, Mistress Daisy. She carried the brush, and of her it may be said, her tongue was hung in the middle and wagged at both ends. Following these came Lady Gertrude and her admirer, Sir Austin Brant, closely watched by Lady Gertrude's stiff and dignified guardian, Mistress Bennett. Then the three suitors of Lady Donovan, Sir Philip Hasty, Sir Harold Hedges and Sir Samuel Davis, who had been devoting themselves as much as was consistent to Lady Helen, Mistress Jessica Joy and Lady Julia.

As the guests greeted their hostess and told of their splendid success, as if from the clouds Arthur Tracy, the jester, appeared among them, and soon had everyone in the best of humor with his fun and nonsense.

Just as all were quieting down, the porter announced that there was a company of players from London at the gate, and that they would be glad to perform if her Ladyship so desired. All cried with one voice for them to be admitted. There was a hasty clearing of everything to one side, and the players were ushered in. There was the renowned Clark Jagger, with his noble air ; and Roy Moore, with his eagle eye ; Floyd Wilson with his awkward gait, Theron Chase and Earl Hamilton with smiles for everyone, and last of all, Deak Mead with his lazy, listless air. The performers arranged themselves and gave the company two very appropriate selections, "The Mouse Trap" and "The Misplaced Kick." Among those who had joined the group after the play began were Father Reasoner, the father confessor of the household, Brother Charles from a nearby Monastery, and Sisters Inez and Theo from a neighboring convent.

After the players were through and the company once more gathered around the great fireplace, Lady Donovan suddenly said to her maidens grouped around her: "Maids, today I had a message from your companion, Nora, and she says she will not return to us, for she is going to share the home of some brave foreign Knight : but she sends to us in her place, a great friend, Mistress Edith Davis." When the excitement over this announcement subsided, the monk began to speak. He said that on his way that day he had stopped at a Gipsy Camp. There he had found four gipsies who gave their names as Lillian, Alice, Mame and Beulah, and they insisted on telling him who he was to meet on his journey. They said that somewhere on the road he would come to two small cottages, in one of which dwelt Mistress Brisbin with her hus-

band and family, and in the other the four celebrated women astrono-
mers, Elsie Hoppham, Lavina Tobin, Mary Martin and Isabella Sidebotham. In another part of his journey he would come upon a partially
deserted Manor House, and that in one part he would find what might
be called Old Maids' Hall. In the hall there lived six spinsters; there
was Mistress Smith, who tended the cats; and Mistress Bird, who sat
in a corner and spun flax; then there was Mistress Osband, who kept
the Hall, cooked the meals and was always happy and cheerful. Besides
the three domestic women there were three intellectual women: Mildred who wrote poetry by the yard; Mistress Newland, who read Greek
all day; and Mistress Green, who amused herself with writing short
romances.

The monk paused and looked thoughtfully into the fire; then rose
abruptly and said it was late and he must go on. But as he spoke, he
raised his arms in benediction and said: "God bless this company! *Sie
sollen leben!*"

CONSTANCE BEMENT.

The Fall of the Alamo

"Give me Liberty, or give me Death!" How many times in the history of the world has the thought contained in these memorable words of Patrick Henry been the key-note of actions which have brought the names of the actors down to posterity, surrounded by a halo of admiration and even reverence!

In Grecian history, 480 years B. C., Leonidas, King of Sparta, and about three hundred of his countrymen held the pass of Thermopylæ against Xerxes' host of three millions until the last man was slain, and for what reason? Simply because they preferred death to slavery among the Persians. The glory of such names grows brighter as the centuries roll along.

But we do not need to go back so far into the history of ages past. Here on our own continent are there not deeds of heroism which are fully as glorious? The bravery of the Pilgrims, who left their homes and native land to brave unknown perils of savage Indians, starvation, and other dangers of an unsettled country, in order to enjoy the liberty of worshiping God in their own way, can scarcely be equaled.

When in 1776 the colonies of America threw off the yoke of the mother country, which had become so burdensome, and declared themselves a free and independent people, Liberty was in universal demand. Liberty they would have, and Liberty they did have in spite of the armed protests of King George. Today, look at the result! The United States has become the grandest nation under the sun!

The example of the United States in thus withdrawing their allegiance to England was copied by many states of America, the most important of which, and the most interesting to us, was Texas. She had long endured, without resistance, the cruel acts of oppression and tyranny passed by Santa Ana, the renowned president of Mexico, who had made himself dictator. But "it is the last straw that breaks the camel's back." He tried one scheme too many by attempting to disarm all the American citizens in Texas, in number about ten thousand. He thus sought to take away that upon which the lives of themselves and families might depend, exposed as they were to warlike Indians. Americans would not submit to such an act, so they headed a revolt against the Mexican government in 1835. From Maine to Florida the news spread on the wings of the wind, and neither money nor soldiers were lacking, for Texas was already considered a part of the Union. A constitutional government was formed and an army provided for, with Gen. Sam Houston as commander-in-chief.

Down in the southern part of Texas is the flourishing town of San Antonio, founded far back in the history of this country. Near by is the fortress of the Alamo, renowned as a second Thermopylae. Hard it is for a visitor now to imagine the scene of desolation and death in this fortress only a little more than fifty years ago. Here were stationed Col. Travis and two hundred men, important among whom were Col. Bowie, and David Crockett, the famous hunter and trapper.

On the first of March, 1836, Santa Ana, at the head of four thousand men, appeared before the Alamo and demanded its surrender. A cannon shot was the answer. Then the bombardment began, and for three days the conflict raged almost without cessation. On the third day Col. Travis, seeing that no help could get to them now, although he had sent messages repeatedly, telling of his difficult situation, called his men together, for the last time, and gave them a chance to choose their manner of death, for death was certain. To a man they stepped across the line which he had drawn, and declared they would die in defense of the Alamo. Even the sick and wounded begged to be carried across the line that they might be joined with their companions. Scarcely were the men arranged when again the battle began, and until the night before the sixth of March the wearied defenders had no rest. On this night all was quiet, save for an unaccountable bustle in the camp of the enemy. At three o'clock in the morning there was a sudden movement among the Mexican ranks. Slowly and silently they crept forward, scaling ladders in readiness. Where are the sentries? Why do they not give the alarm? The ladders are against the wall; up swarm scores of men, but as the heads of the foremost appear, a volley from a hundred rifles rings out. As many of the foes fall before the sure and steady aim of the noble patriots. But with odds twenty to one against them the result is certain; slowly and in good order the defenders withdraw into the main part of the fortress, where they will make their last stand. All know that death is near at hand, but no murmur is heard against the tardy reinforcements; their thoughts are of their homes and their God. It is only a sort of outwork that the Mexicans have gained, but it encourages them to still greater efforts. Onward they rush, over the wall they come, and upon the devoted band pour volley after volley, but those who remain continue to fire with the same steadiness and coolness that made them so feared among their enemies. For six long hours the hand-to-hand conflict rages, even the wounded in the hospital firing upon their foes until their own lives are destroyed by the sword or pistol of one of their blood-thirsty enemies. Staunch and true to the last, Col. Travis and David Crockett fight side by side until both find the death they preferred to slavery and oppression.

> " They come—like autumn leaves they fall,
>   Yet hordes on hordes they onward rush;
> With gory tramp they mount the wall,
>   Till numbers the defenders crush.
>
> The last was felled, the fight to gain;
>   Well may the ruffians quake to tell
> How Travis and his hundred fell
>   Amid a thousand foemen slain.
>
> They died the Spartan's death,
>   But not in hopeless strife;
> Like brothers died, and their expiring breath
>   Was Freedom's breath of life."

The news was quickly spread through Texas, and a spirit of revenge was aroused in the hearts of the patriots, but this was changed to rage against their foes when they heard of the slaughter of 412 American prisoners, who had surrendered at Goliad on the condition that they should be treated as prisoners of war are treated by civilized nations. *Every one of them was shot!* This shows truly the result of the youthful training of the Spanish people in watching scenes of cruelty worthy of a Caligula. Less than a month later there was a reckoning. On April 21,

1836, Gen. Houston, with only 300 men, met Santa Ana on the banks of the San Jacinto River, and there the fury of the Texans, fighting for independence, and their homes and families they loved so well, won the day with odds five to one against them. "Remember the Alamo and Goliad," was their battle-cry, and when the Mexicans heard the fury of that shout their line wavered for an instant. Like a whirlwind the troops of the patriots rushed upon them, swept them from their feet, and the whole Mexican line was in a complete rout. Far and wide they were scattered over the plain, closely pursued by the furious Texans, until at last, wearied out, the Mexicans begged for quarter.

Like civilized people and true Americans, the Texans gave them good treatment in return for the cruel murder of their countrymen. Santa Ana himself was captured, and finally recognized the Republic of Texas, and in 1844 she entered the Union.

At last Texas was free, but at what a cost! Almost a thousand men perished on the Texan side alone during the struggle. Is it worth all it cost? "Yes!" cry the spirits of Travis, Bowie and Crockett. "Had we a thousand lives we would give them all for the cause of liberty." "Yes!" shouts the American volunteer of today as he goes forth to death, perhaps, but still with undaunted valor, to the tune of "The Star Spangled Banner" or "America." "Yes!" will the youth of the future cry, if their country has need of them, and in their hearts will re-echo the last words that David Crockett wrote: "LIBERTY AND INDEPENDENCE FOREVER!"

ARTHUR T. REASONER.

The Unseen Heroic

Song, story and the history of all nations furnish examples of heroic lives. For instance, those of such men and women as Caesar, Napoleon, Joan of Arc, Florence Nightingale and countless others. Their heroism is presented in many different forms—military, political and religious, or in some great service rendered to humanity. Yet, those whom the world applauds are not the greatest heroes. Pages of history reveal the splendor and the beauty of these prominent lives, furnishing inspiration to the youth of today.

But not so well known are many glorious lives of self-sacrifice, high, noble purpose, and consecrated duty. Without notice or applause they have glided by, receiving no reward except the gratitude and love of those with whom they came in contact, and the self-satisfaction of service well performed. The world could ill spare them, for they touch those of every class, rank and condition with a mild and gentle influence. If, then, we judge such men and women as the most heroic, what shall be our standard of heroism?

In the early centuries the main element of heroism was physical force. A single great achievement made a man a hero. Fortitude and courage on the field of battle or in the face of death were indeed heroic, but the man who was bravest in such circumstances was often the greatest coward from a moral point of view.

The hero is not always the one who receives the greatest applause or who has splendid opportunities. When a wealthy man has endowed a college, built a church, or given money for some good purpose, he is rightly spoken of with honor but cannot be called heroic. Neither would that teacher or mother be a hero, who gives time and thought to little children wholly from a feeling of duty. Heroism is not in helping fellowmen simply from a sense of duty or in a way which demands no sacrifice, but by linking our lives with theirs and serving them from love and a wish for their improvement. Is it not this which inspires missionaries to leave home and friends for foreign lands to endure privation and loneliness among uncivilized people? Was it not this spirit which gave the Sisters of Charity strength and determination to leave home for a distant and lonely isle in the Pacific ocean to work and live for the lepers there in banishment?

The hero is not necessarily one of the world's fortunate beings, but the one who has been through "the silent battles, which know the fiercest struggle," and who is ever self-forgetful in the needs of others, seeking the field where "no special greatness breaks the dull tumult of the strife."

The self-considerate are not among the heroes. Who would consider the ultra fashionable man or woman who makes amusement and pleasure a vocation, a hero? Self-sacrifice is indispensable in the truly heroic and is the foremost element in "unseen heroism." Self-sacrifice and unselfishness characterize the highest type of manhood and womanhood. The more a man gives himself to the service of others, the more he forgets self—the more noble he becomes. It is said that in war a soldier is often so devoted to his cause and love for country and home that, in numberless instances, wounds received are unnoticed until from sheer exhaustion he sinks to the ground and is carried from the field. He who is faithful and loyal is most deserving. The true hero has unshaken belief in his cause, whether great or small; he stands firm and confident even in face of defeat. He who is truly courageous understands his motive. A clear conception of the right gives power to resist the appeal of that which will be detrimental to the life.

> "The bravest battle that ever was fought.
> Shall I tell you where and when?
> On the maps of the world you'll find it not—
> 'T was fought by the mothers of men."

What better example can be found of unseen heroism than among the noble, self-denying mothers of our country? Daily toil amidst privation and want to support a family of children. Sacrifices of the necessaries of life to their wants. Such heroic women have brought up famous men. The mention of the mothers of Garfield and Lincoln.

our martyred presidents, recalls to us lives filled with self-denial and unselfishness. There are noble, self-sacrificing mothers in every part of our land who have helped inestimably to form a high standard of heroism. Imagine a soldier without enthusiasm or anyone who has no deep interest in his work; what is his worth? In order to have the arrow hit the mark there must be a firm, strong tension on the bow. No life has succeeded which does not have enthusiasm back of it to furnish inspiration and give it strength and vigor.

A thrilling incident in the great Windsor hotel fire illustrates the combination of those qualities which make a hero ready for an emergency. Warren Guion, in charge of the elevator, persisted in running it until he was taken out by main force, only to rush back and perish at his duty. He had first the desire to serve others, next the courage and perseverance, and finally fidelity to his work. This man was one of the world's unseen heroes, and although such opportunities do not come to all, yet all may possess the characteristics which ennobled him. His were the traits which gave him discretion and readiness to act; although no one would have blamed him if he had first considered self.

In the quiet retirement of the home life are frequently developed the qualities which bloom into heroism under the sunshine of destiny. In the service which preserves the unity and harmony of the home is bred the desire to aid in the happiness of others. In this small circle the greatest heroism may thrive and influences will grow which may stimulate the whole world. The father and mother who labor daily for the welfare of children in school or college are heroic in their self-denial, and inspire their own characteristics in the child. The student who painfully works his way through school or college; who, though insulted, does not retaliate; who, though accustomed to jeers and dislike, can still be gentle and courteous, meeting failure and disappointment with an amiability superior to any of his fellows, is truly noble.

In the cities of our country is felt the influence of the unseen hero. The sick are attended, the poor benefited, tenement houses improved, just laws are made, and much done for the improvement of the condition of the people. Such lives are worthy of imitation and are inspiration to higher service. When we read of the humble devotion of these lives we are thrilled and there comes a desire to emulate their examples and attain their reward. Then we stop to consider what their rewards are. Accustomed to looking on the material side, the most apparent recompense seems to be fame. But the unseen hero's reward is enduring and genuine, for it is that high nobility of character which can only be obtained through self-forgetfulness, sympathy and love for one's fellowmen. The life's capacity has been enlarged, and there is an opportunity for larger growth; there is a self-satisfaction and joy in noble accomplishment which no one can remove. This high nobility of character increases self-respect and lends dignity to each endeavor.

The degree in which each life attains true heroism is dependent upon the individual. Counting his own life dear does not bring happiness or success to a man, but on the contrary these come from his duty to live for others.

This is the era for the true hero, as a time of peace has higher tests of true manhood than ever in war. We are the ones chosen for the unseen heroes of peace.

> " Let us do our work as well,
>   But the unseen and the seen
> Make the house where gods may dwell
>   Beautiful entire and clean."

MILDRED L. KOONSMAN.

Class Work

Editor's Note. The next two articles are from the English classes. We publish them as a sample of English composition because we wish those who are interested in our school work to know what our students are able to do at off-hand writing.

HOW SAMUEL HEZEKIAH ALEXANDER WAS CURED OF A BAD HABIT

Once, a long time ago (of course, we never have such boys now), there lived a very mischievous little boy named Samuel Hezekiah Alexander. He was short and fat, and had red hair. Samuel was noted for his stubby, freckled nose, which was always poking itself where it had no business to be. His eyes, sparkling with fun, were an almost indescribable color, anywhere from blue to green. Although a mischievous, fun-loving lad, he was very polite and a good boy in almost every way.

But he had one very bad fault, and that was telling lies. His mother tried in every way she could imagine to break him of this, but it seemed a hopeless task.

*   *   *   *   *   *

It was the day before Thanksgiving. Many were the mysterious noises throughout the house, especially in the kitchen and pantry.

There was to be a big family dinner at the Alexanders', and the guests had already begun to arrive. Sammy was brimming full of excitement, and went around trying, with his inquisitive nose, to find out what was going on in the kitchen.

Finally his mother said: "Samuel, I haven't time to amuse you, so do run away and play, or you'll certainly drive me crazy;" so Samuel went into the yard and sat down to listen and try to guess what they were doing inside. "I wonder who that can be?" he said to himself, as a carriage appeared in the road. "Why, they're stopping here!" He did not wait to see, but ran to the gate, and who should he meet but his Aunt Jane and three cousins from New York, who, to the great disappointment of the rest, had written that they thought it would be impossible to be with them that year.

Sammy took them into the house and was very polite, but was left to himself again when his mother came in. He stole around by the kitchen door, and oh! the odor of good things that came from inside. He could stand it no longer, and crept softly in, and what a sight met his eyes! There on the pantry shelves were ten pies all in a row, just his favorite kind, and looking around he saw turkeys and all the good things which are seen at such a time.

In a minute a part of a pie had disappeared, and more was about to follow when he happened to think it would be great fun to treat some other boys, so in a second he was off and soon was back again with three of his friends, who were as mischievous as Sam himself. Of course, you know what they did, and then they all ran away as fast as their legs could carry them, for they knew they had been very naughty.

Thanksgiving morning dawned bright and sunny, bringing happiness to every heart. The uncles, aunts, cousins, nephews and nieces began coming early, and eleven o'clock welcomed the last arrival at the Alexander home.

Sammy was lively, as usual, and kept them all laughing, but he didn't feel just right someway. Perhaps it was the pie, but I rather think it was something else; don't you?

It was almost dinner time, when Mrs. Alexander came in and amazed them all by saying sternly: "Samuel Hezekiah Alexander, come here." "Why, ma, what is the matter?" he asked in an astonished, but rather frightened, tone. "Do you know what has become of four mince pies that were in the pantry?" "Mince pies! I haven't seen any," replied Sam. "Well, I know, for I saw four boys eating them yesterday, and since you have told this lie I will have to punish you in a way which you will never forget." Oh! if the floor would only open and let him through. His mother went into the kitchen and soon returned with some soft soap, with which she washed out his mouth. And before all those people, too! He ran right up stairs and had a good cry, and thought it all over. He stayed there half the afternoon. It was very hard, thinking of all the fun down-stairs and that he had no part in it. His mother thought it would be better if she let him have time to think about it, and so did not call him, but after a while a little boy crept softly down-stairs and had a nice little talk with mamma about it. He soon joined the rest, who were having a gay time, and felt so much better that he and all the others forgot that anything had happened.

The evening passed quickly in games, and to bring the day to a happy close a jolly sleigh-ride followed.

That night a tired but happy boy laid his weary head on the pillow, but he felt "all right inside," as he expressed it, and was soon off to Dreamland.

Sammy has grown to be a man now, and often says that day was the most important of his life, for it cured him of his worst fault.

GRACE WHITELEY.

The Butterfly's Ball

Beautiful Miss Goldia Butterfly, the belle of the season, was the only and charming daughter of Hon. Machaon Butterfly, who lived in an aristocratic suburb of Insectville. It was a day of great importance among the higher social circles when Miss Butterfly gave a grand ball.

Miss Butterfly, attired in a becoming yellow silk, received her guests in the spacious drawing rooms, which were profusely decorated with flowers, the color scheme of which was green and white. The tapestry and curtains were tinted autumn leaves. A thick, velvety, green carpet covered the floor.

The first of the company to arrive were her cousins, Royal and Peacock Butterfly, who wore their favorite shades of purple and blue. The next to come were young Mr. and Mrs. Spider, each wearing black velvet trimmed with gold lace. When the Misses Fly heard that the Spiders were invited they sent their regrets, on account of a feud which has long existed between the two families. The young Grasshoppers soon appeared, as lively as usual, getting off their dry jokes. Mr. Beetle, a gallant youth just returned from Paris, entered in all his glory, escorting Miss Katherine Did, familiarly known as Katy Did among her intimate friends. She felt very important arrayed in her green silk gown with point lace sleeves. The smart young Mosquitoes, who were members of the College Glee Club, were present. Although they are very musical and social, they have the disagreeable habit of prying into other people's affairs. The dainty Misses Moth in their white chiffon looked very fairy-like. Miss Butterfly felt obliged to invite Mr. Wasp, an old batchelor, but feared he might hurt someone's feelings because of his sharp tongue. The Misses Honey Bee brought their cousin, Mr. Bumble Bee, a gay, dashing young fellow, who was very attentive to all the ladies. The bright Misses Fire Fly shone like stars in the company.

The Hornets, just home from war, came in full dress uniform, and were very conspicuous in their yellow jackets.

When the Cricket Orchestra started up with lively strains, all the guests joined in the dance, led by the Grasshoppers. Mr. Beetle danced with Miss Katherine Did each number, but Mr. Bumble Bee hummed about among all the ladies. Miss Butterfly and her cousins were very graceful dancers and were much admired.

When the dancing ceased the guests were seated at mushroom tables spread with snowy Easter Lily and fringed Chrysanthemum petals. A delicious menu was served on Rose-leaf plates and in Butter-cups Sweet Peas with Nasturtium salad, honey from the most fragrant flowers, and Dew Drops in Lily-of-the-Valley cups, composed the first course. Snow-berry ices, Heliotrope cake, the richest nectar from the English Violets, and Forget-me-not bonbons were much enjoyed by the guests.

They retired after a few more numbers by the orchestra.

CARRIE WARREN.

The Boy Graduate

"Ye who listen with credulity to the whispers of fancy and pursue with eagerness the phantoms of hope, who expect that age will perform the promises of youth, and that the deficiences of the present will be supplied by the morrow, attend to the history of the" Boy Graduate.

June, the month which ushers in the summer, also brings before the public that necessary adjunct of all educational institutions, the graduating class. A graduating class is always interesting; their interest, speaking of an individual class, is generally local, but the phenomenon taken in its entirety commands an attention which is national, for the graduating class is the culmination of that pride and bulwark of the Republic, the American Common School.

School boards doubtless originated and sustain -have perpetuated the idea of graduating ceremonies and a public presentation of diplomas then the sapient youth, arranged in neat rows and arrayed in new clothes, surrounded by fond parents and kind counselors, listens to a judicious blending of advice and encouragement, receives his diploma and is officially launched on the sea of life. Every effort is made to impress upon his mind the fact that at last he has accomplished something tangible, something that will be of use to him in after life, and while the diploma has no intrinsic value, or fiat value either; and though it possesses no magical properties to conjure the genii of success when rubbed, and though it is not the open sesame to prosperity, still if the bearer will make use of the knowledge the diploma certifies he has, together with the training he must necessarily have acquired-backed by good sense and his own energy, he will have an appreciable advantage in after life. The diploma is in fact like potential energy, and means work done.

While all over the country graduating classes are bursting into bloom with the roses, newspapers are filled with praises of, and poems about, the sweet girl graduate. In spite of the proverb, dear to our

Principal, that the young men should come to the front, the young man, with a keen appreciation of the eternal fitness of things, relegates himself to the background. Believing that the subject, though unimportant, still might have a slight interest, also that it was one to which anyone could easily do full justice, I have chosen the subject of the Boy Graduate; so let it be understood that wherever the term graduate is used, it refers only to that part of the class which predominates on the north side of the Senior assembly room. Although realizing and regretting that I have been forced to take this one-sided, or north-sided, view, I can offer the excuse that I lack that acquaintance with the other side of the subject which would be necessary to do it justice.

Two widely differing views are generally held concerning the High School graduate; first, that he leaves school with a humiliating sense of his own insignificance; the second, and most popular, is that he holds an exaggerated opinion of his importance and abilities. The chief difference between these two views is that both are true; one view might apply to some, and the other to others; but as it is largely a matter of personality, and there is no accounting for personality, it would be hard to determine what proportion of graduates are afflicted with either of these ideas. Perhaps a happy medium may be found between these two extremes which might stand for all the High School is supposed to do for the graduates.

Consider first the graduate with inflated ideas. He leaves school with easy self-assurance, knowing intuitively that the gates of success will not remain barred against such as he; his way will not be hard, for has he not worked hard for four or five years that he may have smooth sailing the rest of his life? But beneath this complacency there is one great fear—suppose his talents should be misdirected! What a world wide calamity that would be—a second Pitt, a Raphael, a Napoleon, or a Washington, born to waste their greatness on the desert air. He is keenly conscious of the tremendous responsibility resting on his shoulders, and he willingly turns from the appalling thought to bask in the sunshine of his own bright prospects.

A graduate with an adequate appreciation of his own insignificance would be so contrary to human nature as to be a monstrosity, and probably the idea that there are such is held simply to offset the other extreme. But of the scholar who leaves school with but little faith in himself and still less in the world, doubtful of his own talents and of others' ability, mistaking me′di′o′cre attainments for worthy effort, vacillating always, and everywhere evasive, of a "here today and away tomorrow" cast of character, idly waiting for the fickle wind of chance to start him on the path he has neither the courage nor inclination to select himself, but little need be said, for his story is old and his fate is certain. Of this species let us hope there are few. Thriving on insecurity and delay, they are everywhere a hindrance and a discord, for that which mars their school career will mark their after life.

Now look at the graduate who leaves school conscious that he has seized and made use of every opportunity, that he has performed every duty well, who has learned aside from book knowledge those equally important lessons of self-restraint, respect for authority, perseverance and punctuality, the last of which alone is of incalculable benefit. Such a graduate is ready for life; ready to find his place and fill it, willing to take advice and give help, believing that "there is always work and tools to work withal for those who will," and possessed of a stable mental and moral equilibrium, he will have all the advantages of a good start in life's journey. No fear may be felt that such a graduate, removed from the fraternal atmosphere of school, will shrink from his duty in after life. With confidence his diploma may say to him:

"Take up the young man's burden, have done with childish days,
The praise of friend and kindred, the doubts that many raise;
By all ye say or promise, by all ye try or do,
The cold, unbiased world shall weigh your deeds and you."

However much the utility of the High School studies may be questioned, there can be no question of the benefit derived from what are supposed to be side issues, but which are really (to use a common expression) alone worth the price of admission. Perseverance is worth more than Physics, and self-restraint than Grammar Review. It is these lessons well learned that mean success, for success will surely be with him who exercises in after life those qualities which make one's way smooth in the L. H. S. First and foremost punctuality, a perseverance which knows no barrier, straight-forwardness, and honesty of purpose, a respect for authority, and a cheerful self-restraint, a slight sprinkling of ability, and the unconquerable will, and courage never to submit and yield. But then, "A boy's will is the wind's will, and the thoughts of youth are long, long thoughts."

DRAKE MEADE.

High Standard of Scholarship

At a college in a city far away, instead of being required to take a written examination, the person who applies for entrance passes, first, before a board of examiners, consisting of five members, each one of whom plies the student with a few questions, and then before the chaplain of the college, and if these questions are satisfactorily answered the applicant is allowed to enter unconditionally.

In the autumn of 1899 a student stands prepared to undergo this oral quiz. By his confident manner and "know-it-all" air, as also by the following interview, we can easily recognize him as a graduate of that illustrious class, the class of '99, L. H. S.

Examiner No. I begins: "Let me see, Mr. A. During your Senior year you studied English Literature, Physics, German, Latin, Reviews, etc. Please tell me what you learned of the life of Johnson; some 'pivotal' point about which you are going to group all the other facts of his life." The student answers: "At the age of twenty-six Mr. Johnson married a fleshy, gaudy widow of forty-eight years." "Very good; and now what do you remember of the life of Scott?" Answer: "On leaving church one rainy day Mr. Scott espied a pretty, young maid without any umbrella. He offered to share his with her; fell desperately in love; but the fair Margaret rejected him." No. I exclaims: "A remarkable memory! You may enter the English class. I am satisfied."

Now steps forward Examiner No. II. "Ah, my young man, and what does your copious memory retain of your Physics lessons?" Then comes the quick response: "Many important facts about Physics come surging to my mind, but foremost comes the thought of the day when our teacher demonstrated to us the use of the phonograph and gramophone. I can also recall very vividly the day that Mr. Willey sent a young man from class for chewing gum."

Examiner No. II is highly elated and steps back to make room for No. III. No. III comes forward. "During the last semester of your Senior year you reviewed Arithmetic, Grammar and Algebra, did you not, Mr. A? Tell us, please, what recollections you have of these studies." With a smile the student(?) replies: "In grammar I learned from Harold that a goatee is a little goat. Of Arithmetic I most plainly remember Mr. Smith's apology to the chair for having knocked it over, and my recollections of Algebra can be represented by the unknown quantity—X."

After making several complimentary remarks, No. III withdraws and No. IV comes up, rubbing his hands with a self-satisfied air. He reviews the student on his knowledge of the languages and learns that Mr. A's capacity for remembering is as great and as remarkable along this line as on other subjects. He fondly recalls the pleasant hours spent in translating German in the Physical laboratory far down in the cellar, and also the time spent with his beloved Virgil far up in the attic. He has not forgotten his struggles with Greek nor how much chocolate fudge aids in translating it.

Since Examiners Nos. I, II, III and IV having already proved the great extent of the young man's learning, No. V takes it upon himself to question him about the characteristics of his graduating class, to which the student replies: "Our class was always known as the original class, having been the first to introduce the Sophomore Ex., the first to adopt the extensive use of nose-classes, and was also noted for their extremely quiet class-meetings."

Although the youth is pretty well tired by this time, he does not fail to notice the great admiration and respect with which he is looked upon by the Board, and so, when the chaplain comes up, he greets him with a smile and gives respectful attention to what the reverend gentleman has to say to him. After inquiring of what church he was a member and what his religious views were, the chaplain asks him to give a brief review of the last sermon he heard. This is the reply: "The minister gave a fine sermon on the study of the Bible, but what impressed me most was this story he told: A Methodist, who had a melancholy disposition, was accustomed to go to the Bible for comfort. He would open the Bible at random, place his finger on some text and maintained that this text had a special meaning for him. One day, feeling very despondent, he went to his Bible, opened it thus, and the words which he read were: 'And Judas went forth and hanged himself.' Not finding any comfort in this, he closed the book, opened it again and read these words: 'Go thou and do likewise.'"

With one accord the Board of Examiners agree that the young man has a great capacity for learning (more) and gladly place his name on the college enrollment list.

FLORENCE GREEN.

Along the Bay of Naples

To the lover of scenery and antiquity there is, perhaps, no place more interesting on this earth than Naples and its surroundings.

The bay of Naples is the most beautiful in the world. The green slopes of Posillipo, the precipitous cliffs of the Sorrentine mainland, the purple mountains covered with groves of orange and lemon, the domed city nestling against the hillsides, and the burning mountain form a picture unsurpassed in beauty, and one never to be forgotten.

And it is not less grand from the view of a lover of antiquity. Here, guarded by the grim sentinel, Vesuvius, lie the buried cities of Pompeii and Herculaneum with their relics of Roman civilization. The mountain sides surrounding the bay are covered with the ruins of Roman villas, baths and castles.

It was a beautiful May morning when an American friend and myself mounted our bicycles for a visit to the neighboting cities of Baia and Pozzuoli with their old Roman ruins. Our road leads up the hill of Posillipo, which separates Naples from the Bay of Baia. We have left the busy city behind us and are riding between groves of olive and orange. We pass many beautiful summer homes hidden in bowers of tropical vegetation. Our road becomes steeper, and after a few minutes of hard pedaling we reach level ground. We pass through a narrow defile in the rocks and then, turning a sharp curve in the road, we behold a picture of beauty. We are gazing on the beautiful Bay of Baia, dotted with numerous vine-clad islands. At the bottom of the hillside we see vineyards and olive groves. To our right extends a mountain range of extinct volcanoes, and in the distance, reaching into the sea like a huge arm, the promontory of Misenum. We stop but a moment to gaze upon the scene, and are soon coasting along the zigzag road down the hillside.

Our road now leads along the sea shore. Quaintly garbed, barefooted fishermen are pulling in their nets or fixing their boats. In the distance we see fishing villages and fleets of white-winged boats.

We pass through the little town of Bagnoli, so-called on account of its numerous bathing establishments. We ride on farther and farther; the outlines of the promontory of Misenum become more distinct. We pass an Italian prison guarded by soldiers, and then, making a sharp turn, we see situated on an eminence extending into the sea the town of Pozzuoli, or the ancient Puteoli of the Bible. In the days of the Roman empire it was a flourishing Roman city and boasted of many rich summer villas. Here St. Paul landed from the good ship " Castor and Pollux " and tarried on his journey to Rome. It was from here that Caligula built a bridge across the bay to Baia, a distance of over three miles. The bridge was built of boats covered with earth, and Caligula crossed and recrossed for three days. We visit the temple of the Egyptian god, Serapis, the only temple of its kind in Italy. Its main features are three Corinthian columns of Egyptian granite which are forty feet high. There is undoubtedly a connection between this temple and the sea, for in stormy weather the court of the temple is full of water which rises from below. The temple was probably under water for centuries, for one can see where shell fish have eaten away the bases of the columns. From here we go to the amphitheatre, one of the best preserved in Italy. We are shown beneath the arena, the dungeons where the wild beasts were kept, and also see the dungeon where St. Januarius (the patron saint of Naples) was imprisoned before he was thrown to the wild beasts. It is said that the animals would not harm him, and that he was beheaded afterwards a short distance from the city.

We inspect the arena, climb around the deserted seats, and after getting a fine view from the top, set out for the Solfatara.

The Solfatara is a crater of an almost extinct volcano, which commands a magnificent view of the surrounding country. The crater is surrounded by hills covered by volcanic ashes and sulphur. Sulphuric gases rise from the ground and at times we hear faint rumblings beneath us. The whole crater is covered by a white material resembling clay. After collecting several pieces of the volcanic formation covered with crystals of sulphur, we return to the city. We are getting rather hungry, and, after diligent searching, find a picturesque restaurant situated on a rock projecting into the sea. Here we regale ourselves with macaroni with tomato sauce, fried alice (a fish resembling our sardines) with fried potatoes, and for a last course, oranges, lemons and finocchio. After dinner we take a walk around the town, gaze at the narrow streets and old stone houses, and then set out for Baia. We leave the road along the sea shore and take an ascending road which leads inland.

On both sides of the road are hills covered with vineyards which hide from us all view of the surrounding country. The road is so steep that we are compelled to walk most of the way. Suddenly the hills on one side cease, and we see below us, like an arena in an amphitheatre of hills, the lake Avernus. This lake, in ancient times, was surrounded by impenetrable forests, sulphuric vapors arose from fissures in the ground, and the people regarded it with awe. The scene before us is one of solemn grandeur; to the right Mount Gaurus rears its heights and in the distance lies the blue Mediterranean and the Lucrine Lake.

We see close to the water's edge the grotto of the Cumæn Sybyl and the entrance to the Infernal Regions almost hidden by luxuriant vineyards. We rest here but a moment and then ride on towards Cumæ. We ride under a huge arch (63 feet high) extending from one side of the ravine to the other. It is made of thin Roman brick and was the supporting arch of an ancient Roman aqueduct. Before and beyond us we see, marked by a few uncertain ruins, the city of ancient Cumæ.

We pass the Lago Fusaro, the famous oyster beds of the ancient Romans, beneath whose waters you may still see the rich mosaics of a Roman palace. Before us rises a long range of hills and passing through a short valley we reach Baia. We have reached now the most interesting part of our journey, the city of Baia, the once famous Roman stronghold. Here were the magnificent summer homes of the rich Romans, who, on account of the beautiful bay and its scenery and balmy climate, preferred this city to all others.

It was also renowned from its warm mineral springs which abound here. Now, however, the only evidence of this city's former grandeur are the old ruins crowning the hillsides. We visit the beautiful temples of Venus, Diana and Mercury and a few fishers' huts by the deserted seaside.

As we pass through the narrow streets dark featured boys and girls run after us clamoring for "soldi" (pennies) or importuning us to buy old bits of marble and mosaics which they have found in some ruin. Before many houses we see young girls spinning flax, and through some doorways we see old-fashioned looms at work.

Near the little village of Bacoli, so-called from the villa Bauli, where Nero murdered his mother, we visit some subterranean ruins, called the "Cento Camerelle" or the labyrinth, which were probably the substructions of Julius Cæsar's villa. By the aid of torches we grope our way through innumerable damp chambers of stone. From here we go to the Piscina Mirabilis, the reservoir which in ancient times contained the water for the Roman fleet. It is a huge under-ground structure supported by forty-eight mammoth columns. A short distance beyond we see some old ruins, the tomb of Agrippina, Nero's mother. On stormiest nights, when all the furies of the darkest realms are abroad, you may still see walking on the troubled waters of the bay the white robed form of the murdered queen.

It was moonlight when we returned to Naples, and who could ever forget that ride along the silver sea washed shores, amid the phantoms of the long ago?

We pass the ruins of Cæsar's palace, the baths of Nero, the villas of Cicero and Petronious bathed in the full moon's shimmering light, and dream as we swiftly whirl along of the departed glories of the Roman empire.

FRED DEAN.

Foot Ball Team

GUY D. SMITH, Manager

HAROLD CHILDS, '01, Captain

Tackles,	{ Right—Herbert Barringer { Left—Clyde Rumsey
Center,	Drury Porter
Fullback,	{ Med Lauzen { Austin Brant
Guards,	{ Rex Plummer { John Harden { Ned Hopkins { Roger Humphry { Henry Baker
Ends,	{ Ray Dillingham { Cameron Hartness { Ford McKarrick { Henry Baker
Halfback,	{ Lorenzo Zimmer { Harold Childs
Quarterback,	Don Childs
Substitute,	Walter Shuttleworth

GAMES

L. H. S. 27, Owosso H. S. 0

L. H. S. 21, Owosso H. S. 0

L. H. S. 5, M. A. C. Second Team 5

L. H. S. 60, Freshmen Team 0

L. H. S. 30, "   " 0

L. H. S. 0, Jackson City Team 17

FOOTBALL TEAM.

"How They Went Away   How They Came Back"

Sing a song of ball games,
    Sing, O sing for fame;
Sing of nine brave fellows
    In a base ball game.

When the game was opened
    They began to sing:
"We'll beat Eaton Rapids,
    'We won't do a thing!'"

When the game was ended
    They began to sing:
"You've the prize, we grant it —
    We've not done a thing."

Sing a song of ball games,
    Sing you not of blame;
For the High School Ball Team's
    "All right," just the same.

Base Ball Team

OFFICERS

JAMES PORTER, '99, Manager

JOHN FRASER, '99, Captain

Pitcher,	John Chapman, '99
Catcher,	Adelbert Baker, '99
First Base,	Dell Moon, '00
Second Base,	Albert Fraser, '00
Short Stop,	Judson Lyon, '02
Third Base,	Ralph Holdridge, '02
Left Field,	Harold McKale, '00
Center Field,	John Fraser, '99
Right Field,	Clyde Rumsey, '01
Substitutes,	Floyd Wilson / Asa Beverly

RECORD

Owosso High School,	Twelve to three
Second Team, M. A. C.,	Seven to six
First Team, M. A. C.,	Nine to eight
Eaton Rapids,	Eight to eighteen
Alumni,	Thirty to two

BASEBALL TEAM.

Records of the Michigan Inter-Scholastic Athletic Association, '95 to '99

100 yard dash—Christopher, Lansing, at Jackson, '95: 10 2-5 seconds.

220 yard dash- Ellis, Detroit, at Ann Arbor, '99; 23 seconds.

440 yard dash—Christopher, Lansing, at Jackson, '95: 53 3-5 seconds.

Half-mile run—Dayrell, Grand Rapids, at Lansing, '96: 2 minutes 14 seconds.

Mile run—Barlow, Greenville, at Ann Arbor, '99: 5 minutes 4 2-5 seconds.

120 yard hurdles—Cole, Lansing, at Ann Arbor, '97: 18 seconds.

220 yard hurdles –Christopher, Lansing, at Ann Arbor, '98: 28 2-5 seconds.

Mile walk Standish, Detroit, at Ann Arbor, '98: 9 minutes 13 1-5 seconds.

Running high jump Snow, Detroit, at Ann Arbor, '97: 5 feet 8 inches.

Running broad jump Christopher, Lansing, at Lansing, '96: 21 feet 6½ inches.

Pole vault Christopher, Lansing, at Lansing, '96: 9 feet 1 inch.

Throwing 16-pound hammer Lehman, Adrian, at Ann Arbor, '98: distance, 87 feet 5 inches.

Putting 16-pound shot –Forrest, Ann Arbor, at Ann Arbor, '99: 34 feet 10 inches.

Quarter-mile bicycle- Phelps, Grand Rapids, at Lansing, '96: 34 seconds.

Half-mile bicycle Ulp, Ann Arbor, at Lansing, '96: 1 minute 13 seconds.

Mile bicycle Dodds, Detroit, at Ann Arbor, '97: 2 minutes 22 4-5 seconds.

Michigan Inter-Scholastic Field Day

Held at Ann Arbor, May 27 and 28, 1899

The following is a list of the schools entered and points scored:

School.	Points
Detroit, - - - - -	43
Ann Arbor, - - - -	36
Pontiac, - - - - -	16
Adrian, - - - -	15
Mt. Clemens, - - - -	13
Greenville, - - - -	11
Saginaw, West Side, - - -	5
Lansing, - - - -	3
Grand Rapids, - - - -	1
Howell, - - - -	1

EVENTS

100 yard dash—Ellis, Detroit, first; Thompson, Pontiac, second; Ingles, Detroit, third. Time, 11 3-5.

220 yard dash -Ellis, Detroit, first; Thompson, Pontiac, second; Tucker, Ann Arbor, third. Time, 23.

440 yard dash—Coon, Ann Arbor, first; Finch, Adrian, second; Baker, Detroit, third. Time, 58 4-5.

880 yard run—Dubois, Ann Arbor, first; Barlow, Greenville, second; Avery, Howell, third. Time, 2:18 3 5.

Mile run Barlow, Greenville, first; Whitelock, Ann Arbor, second; Hitchman, Detroit, third. Time, 5:04 2-5.

Mile walk—Perry, Ann Arbor, first; Kinyon, Ann Arbor, second, Lindwall, Adrian, third. Time, 9:18.

120 yard hurdles—Tucker, Ann Arbor, first; Standish, Detroit; second; Shotwell, Detroit, third. Time, 19 1-5.

220 yard hurdles--Dawson, Pontiac, first; James, Detroit, second; Crane, Grand Rapids, third. Time, 29 4-5.

Running broad jump—Ellis, Detroit, first; Thompson, Pontiac, second; Osborne, Detroit, third. Distance, 20 feet 8 inches.

Running high jump Ellis, Detroit, first; Barlow, Greenville, second; Dawson, Pontiac, third. Height, 5 feet 3 inches.

Pole vault- -Seiffer, Adrian, first; Osborne, Detroit, second; Woodrow, Ann Arbor, third. Height, 9 feet.

Hammer throw Reibling, Detroit, first; Childs, Lansing, second; Wilcox, Adrian, third. Distance, 76 feet 4 inches.

Shot put—Forrest, Ann Arbor, first; Sims, Ann Arbor, second; Hughs, Pontiac, third. Distance, 34 feet 10 inches.

TRACK TEAM.

HAROLD CHILDS   HENRY BAKER   WALTER SHUTTLEWORTH   NED LATZEN
Manager and Captain   FORD McKABRICK   LANCE THORNE
REX PLUMMER   CAMERON HARTNESS   TRACY McCULLEY

Senior Banquet

"Hunger is a cloud out of which falls a rain of eloquence and knowledge."

At K. O. T. M. Hall, June 20, 1899

MENU

Roast Chicken
Green Peas   Mashed Potatoes
Bread and Butter
Pickles   Celery   Olives
Salted Almonds
Waldorf Salad   Cheese Straws
Fancy Ice Cream   Cake
Coffee

Music by Baker & Wescott.

Toasts

DRAKE MEADE, Toastmaster

The gentleman is learned and a most rare speaker.

The Faculty,   -   -   -   -   -   -   -   -   Mr. Holmes

"All wisdom centers there."

Our Trials,   -   -   -   -   -   -   -   -   Marie Nichols

"If you have tears prepare to shed them now."

Pigmies,   -   -   -   -   -   -   -   -   Arthur Tracy

"What are you good for, my little man?"

Ponies,   -   -   -   -   -   -   -   Mable Hudson

"Listen, my children, and I will tell
Of the wild-eyed steed you know so well."

The Oracle,   -   -   -   -   -   -   Herbert Barringer

"My griefs cry louder than my advertisements."

Music,   -   -   -   -   -   -   -   Miss Lemon

Our Freshmen Days,   -   -   -   -   -   -   Miss King

" How dear to our hearts are the days of our childhood."

The Schoolmaster,   -   -   -   -   -   -   Theoren Chase

"A man he was severe and stern to view."

The Ideal Man,   -   -   -   -   -   -   Edith Davis

"What is a gentleman? It is a thing
Decked in an eye glass, a watch, and a ring."

Ninety-nine,   -   -   -   -   -   -   Earle Hamilton

Enenekonta! Enna!
Right in line!
Lansing High School!
Ninety-nine!

The Seniors,   -   -   -   -   -   -   -   Miss Douglas

"Let none presume to wear an undeserved dignity."

Senior Reception

In honor of the new teachers

Miss Helen Douglas, Miss Grace Smith, Mr. Guy Smith and Miss
Ernestine Robinson

Given at the Church of Our Father, Sept. 30, 1898

Program consisted of a piano duet by Miss Lillian Renner and Miss
Mildred Koonsman and extemporaneous talks.

Annual Junior Reception

in honor of

The Class of 1902

At the Church of Our Father, Oct. 21, 1898

PROGRAM

Vocal Solo - - - - -	Mable Smith
Recitation - -	Lysle Smith
Solo - - - -	Fred Dorsey
Recitation - - - - -	Clark Jagger
Violin Solo - - -	Florence Birdsall

Program

of

Baccalaureate Service

at

Plymouth Congregational Church, Sunday Evening, June 18, 1898

Organ Prelude— Nocturne from "Midsummer Night's Dream,"
                    Mr. Hooker   *Mendelssohn*

Hymn

Prayer

Solo— "Adore and Be Still,"   -   -   -   -   *Gounod*
                Mrs. Edmonds

Scripture Reading

Duet "Hark, Hark My Soul,"   -   -   -   -   *Shelley*
       Mrs. Edmonds and Mr. Atkinson

Sermon—"The Man and the Tool,"
             Rev. Clarence F. Swift

Quartet—"Send Out Thy Light,"   -   -   -   *Gounod*
    Mrs. Edmonds   Mr. Van Buren
      Mrs. Campbell.   Mr. Atkinson

Prayer

Hymn

Benediction

Organ Postlude Verset,   -   -   -   *E. de la Tombelle*
             Mr. Hooker

The Baccalaureate Sermon

REV. CLARENCE F. SWIFT.

It is a unique and valued privilege which is mine tonight to preach to you, members of the Class of 1899, the last sermon which you, as public school scholars, will ever listen to. As you go from the school work to the various activities of your lives, the passing years will bring to you, I trust, many opportunities to listen to abler sermons than this one. I am sure, however, that not one of them will have so many accompanying circumstances to add to its value as this one has, and I know that you will never listen to one which is prompted by a more earnest, prayerful desire to utter some word whose blessing for you shall be real and abiding.

My theme tonight is "The Man and the Tool." My text is Ecclesiastes 10:10:

"If the iron be blunt, and one do not whet the edge, then must he put to more strength: but wisdom is profitable to direct."

Every realm pays its tribute, of illustration, of symbolism, of allegory, to the teacher of moral truth. Sky and earth and sea, mountain and valley, rock and tree and flower, have been drafted into the service. With special readiness, every sphere of human activity makes its liberal contribution to the cause of moral instruction. The king on his throne, the general with his cohorts, the learned judge upon the bench, the shepherd and his flocks, the merchant and his goods, the farmer and his grain, the housewife and her mess of dough, the woodchopper and his axe, all these come to the preacher and offer their services to him as he assumes the duty of uttering a message to the waiting congregation.

I accept, tonight, the service of the last mentioned helper, and ask you to join with me in drawing some truths from the humble, homely, helpful figure of the woodchopper and his axe.

"If the iron be blunt, and one do not whet the edge, then must he put to more strength; but wisdom is profitable to direct."

Wanted, material to enter into the making of useful articles,—timbers for a vessel, lumber for a house, or a box, or a chair. Necessary thereto,—a tree cut down. Means therefor,—a man and an axe. Problem,—the mutual interdependence of the two factors; the duty of the axe to the man, and of the man to the axe.

What a sermon that woodchopper of England, the "Grand Old Man," might have preached on such a theme! But even one who is not a woodchopper can hardly fail to see the pertinence and the directness of the figure as applied to the present circumstance.

Wanted,—years of life transformed into service to humanity, into worthy business and professional careers, into results that shall count for the Kingdom. Means therefor,—some young men and women, possessed of brains and hearts and bodies, with powers whetted to the keen edge of efficiency by years of education; also, a will power, a purpose to wield the instrument. Problem, the mutual interdependence of these two factors: the relation of will-power to discipline and culture and of discipline and culture to will-power.

I am sure that not too much is taken for granted in assuming the presence of these two factors here tonight. Surely, no one will hesitate to indorse the sentiment, "The Class of '99; up to the present time the best in history."

The personal force is here, the purpose, the will, the vital power. The axe is keen-edged, made so by the whetting of these years of discipline and mental culture under the direction of efficient guides and counselors. Results will equal the product of these two factors; richest results will come from the constant co-operation of the two. A purpose kept strong, an edge kept keen, these will compel success and satisfaction.

The first truth which we learn from the woodchopper is that no keen-edged axe will chop a tree, except the axe be wielded.

No boat, though it be the scientific shell for the regatta, constructed to respond to the lightest impulse of the rower, will row itself up stream. No amount of capital will make a successful business career. No splendid machine will run itself. No mental culture and discipline, no equipment of brains and knowledge and ability, will insure a life worth living, except wielded by the purpose and will of the person. We are prone to add to the text a kind of *per contra*, to this effect: "If the iron be sharp, and one keep the edge whetted, then need he put to no strength at all." But the *per contra* is perfectly contrary to all experience. The law is, "No effort, no results." "To reap the harvest, you must sow the seed." A keen-edged axe is an opportunity, an advantage, a way open. Opportunity becomes transmuted into result only when he who has the opportunity adds himself as a moving factor.

There is something sad in the sense of loss to the world suggested by the poet's words:

> "Full many a gem of purest ray serene,
> The dark, unfathomed caves of ocean bear;
> Full many a flower is born to blush unseen,
> And waste its sweetness on the desert air."

In the application of the words we find a sadder feeling still, as we think of the "Village Hampdens" that never withstood the tyrant's oppression, or of the "mute, inglorious Miltons" whose songs never found words. But a new element is added to the feeling of regret, when we remember the untold wealth of learning, of culture, of advantage, by which the world has never been blessed, simply because the purpose was absent to make use of the instrument. Selfishness, laziness, incompetence—these tell the story of many an uncut tree whose material the world sorely needs.

Moreover, since results come as the product of the two factors, then if quality of axe and keenness of edge be assumed as permanent factors, results will vary as effort varies. No effort, no result. Little effort, little result. Large effort, large result.

Let me change the figure of speech for a moment. Over the door of a school house down east somewhere there are graven these words: "Row, not Drift." I think it is easy to teach and enforce that thought when the current sets in the wrong direction and the dangerous rapids are just below. It is easy then to see that drifting means danger, and that one must ply the vigorous oar to offset the perilous power of the current. When circumstances are against us we appreciate the cheering message of a modern poet:

> If you strike a thorn or rose,
>   Keep a-goin'!
> If it hails, or if it snows,
>   Keep a-goin'!
> 'Tain't no use to sit an' whine
> When the fish ain't on your line,
> Bait your hook an' keep on tryin',
>   Keep a-goin'!
>
> When it looks like all is up,
>   Keep a-goin'!
> Drain the sweetness from the cup,
>   Keep a-goin'!
> See the wild birds on the wing,
> Hear the bells that sweetly ring,
> If you feel like singin', sing!
>   Keep a-goin'!

But peril really comes when the current is setting our way, when we are drifting in the direction in which we plan to go; when we are surrounded by advantages, by influences that tend to help us upward and onward. There is a subtle danger in good environment. There is a disadvantage in advantages, and a real advantage in disadvantages·

The following facts are told of the youthful days of William H. Seward: "His father gave him a thousand dollars and told him to go to college and graduate. The son returned at the end of the first year, his money all gone, and with several extravagant habits. At the close of the vacation the judge said to his son, 'Well, William, are you going to college this year?' 'I have no money, father.' 'But I gave you a thousand dollars to graduate on.' 'It is all gone, father.' 'Very well, my son ; it is all I could give you ; you can't stay here ; you must now pay your own way in the world.' A new light broke upon the vision of the young man. He accommodated himself to the situation, again left home, made his way through college, graduated at the head of his class, studied law, became Governor of the State of New York, and entered the Cabinet of the President of the United States."

Advantages do not need to be hindrances, they may be real helps. It all depends upon the person. They are a blessing, if. no matter which way the current sets, you stick to the text and "row, not drift."

Not only does the addition of this new factor increase results, making greater speed as the power of the person is added to the power of the current, but it is only by rowing that the power to row is maintained and developed. No advantages have become a real help to you until they have taught you to do without them. Splints and crutches have their highest mission in guiding the lame man to the point where he can throw them away. Many a help becomes a hindrance because it does away with the necessity for self-help.

Some Frenchmen have been measuring and figuring as to the possibility of tunneling Mont Blanc so that one may reach the summit by elevator in a shaft sunk from the top. But being at the top is only a small part of the fascination of a visit to Mont Blanc. The real pleasure is in the climb, the toil and delight of getting to the top. He who works his way to the top is the one who gets value from the position.

An interesting fact in entomology illustrates this same danger that attaches to advantages. A person interested in the subject had secured a fine specimen of an emperor moth in the larva state. Day by day he watched the little creature as he wove about him his cocoon, which is very singular in shape, much resembling a flask. Presently the time drew near for it to emerge from its wrappings and spread its large wings of exceeding beauty. On reaching the narrow aperture at the neck of the flask, the pity of the person watching it was so awakened to see the struggle necessary to get through that he cut the cords, thus making the passage easier. But, alas! his false tenderness destroyed all the brilliant colors for which this species of moth is noted. The severe pressure was the very thing needed to cause the flow of fluids which create the marvelous hues. Its wings were small, dull in color, and the whole development was imperfect.

Science, poetry, good sense, join in a warning against the subtle dangers lurking in advantages.

The scientist speaks:—"Any new set of conditions occurring to an animal which render its food and safety very easily attained seem to lead, as a rule, to degeneration."

Hear Tennyson's stirring verse:—

> "Life is not an idle ore,
> But iron dug from central gloom,
> And heated hot with burning fears,
> And dipt in baths of hissing tears,
> And battered with the shocks of doom,
>   To shape and use."

And Oliver Wendell Holmes caps it all with these sensible words: "To reach the port of Heaven, we must sail sometimes with the wind and sometimes against it—but we must sail, and not drift, nor lie at anchor."

To state this same truth in the figure of the text, failure to wield the keen edged axe not only denies us the results, but it blunts the edge; not, to be sure, by the honorable blunting of constant use, but by the dishonorable blunting that comes from rust and corroding. Many a man there has been in the world, of brilliant powers, with axe keen edged, whose value was about equal to that of a long abandoned railroad, which was described as consisting of "two streaks of rust and a right of way." Don't let the edge rust away. It makes a lot of extra work to be shiftless. It lightens labor to keep the edge bright by constant use.

It is worthy of mention here that no system of schools in the world does so much to develop a constraining purpose on the part of the person as the one which you have had the benefit of. Germany can teach us some things about schooling, but the German school sharpens the axe and expects an imperial power outside the individual to do the wielding. Our own schools teach this with goodly emphasis: "Wield your own axe."

But more needs to be said now concerning this matter of keeping a keen edge on the axe.

Assuming the unfailing purpose of the person, then results will vary with the bluntness or the keenness of the axe's edge. A blunt edge complicates the problem. The text tells us that a dull axe compels more strength for the same result; that results which can be secured by a normal, moderate use of power with a keen edge, require an abnormal, immoderate exertion with a blunt edge. It means a constant economy of energy to keep the edge whetted. A sharp axe is the great labor saving device.

By the same rule it is clear that with a constant keenness of edge, the extra strength may be devoted to enlarging results. It is much more satisfactory to work harder and see larger results than it is to waste energy in counteracting a dull tool.

We have found that the axe may acquire a rusty bluntness by not being used at all, that mental power and training lose their efficiency by failure to operate. There are two other methods of blunting the edge.

It may be done by an unskilful wielding of the axe. I think the last clause of the text means to assure us that good judgment in the use of a blunt edge will partially offset the lack of keenness; that the lack of mental discipline is not a fatal defect if purpose and wisdom combine to remedy the lack. "Wisdom is profitable to direct" even the unwhetted axe.

But this phrase certainly means also that "wisdom is profitable to direct" the sharpened tool, in order to produce best results and keep from nicking and blunting the edge. There is a great deal of activity in the world that is inefficient in attaining its purpose and harmful in its effect upon equipment, because it lacks that uncommon commodity known as common sense. "Wisdom is profitable to direct."

And what shall we say of that blunting of the edge of the tools of service that comes from the wasting of power on objects false or unworthy or trivial? A trained intellect may be employed to carry on af honorable business, or to manipulate cash accounts for purposes on fraud. A bright mind may be devoted to the promotion of useful industry, or to putting a skilful counterfeit on the market. Splendid powers may be given to splendid ambitions, they may be lowered to uses trivial and mean.

Verily, as when a company of intelligent and cultured men and women, with the finest of well-trained horses and a noble pack of hounds, spend a day in dangerous and exhaustive toil for the brush of one poor little fox, so is it when a man or woman, gifted with powers fit for a high and holy purpose, squanders the precious years of existence in a life of frivolity, seeking to know only this one thing, "how may I amuse myself?" Nothing dulls the edge of power so quickly, robs the life of its energy so surely, as the consciousness of petty, unworthy aims.

Do not misunderstand me. There is a difference between a life of small services, and one of petty purposes.

I remember a visit I once made to a paper mill. I watched the methods by which the wood was chewed into pieces, disintegrated into pulp, and manipulated, by various processes, into paper. The processes and the machinery represent an almost incredible amount of chemical research, of inventive and mechanical skill, of executive ability and invested capital. At the end there is a striped paper sack in which your grocer might send home a pound of crackers. Is all the investment wasted then? Not at all. It is not one sack, but millions of them. Each separate sack is small, but not petty, for it has a real service to render.

Our vast system of education, with all its expense and its demands on time and strength, is no failure if it multiplies the servants of humanity. Many may be obliged to occupy a small place, no one needs to live a petty life.

Be loyal always to your best selves — pure in heart, clean and wholesome in word, unquestioned in business dealing, unstained in reputation. Remember the words of William E. Russell—"There is an everlasting difference between making a life and making a living."

Still another occasion for blunting the edge of efficiency is the too incessant use of the tool of service. Use is good. Wise use is essential. But wise use means now and then a vacation from use. The brain that thinks, the muscle that works, the scythe that cuts, the axe that chops, the very wires that the scientist uses in his experiments—these all have one law, that too constant exertion destroys efficiency. The Sabbath law is not an arbitrary imposition, it is a recognition of the absolute demand of the human mind and body; "The Sabbath was made for man." The hours, the weeks of vacation time are not wasted, they are creating values by storing up energy. Ten months of school and two months of rest net more knowledge than twelve months of school. One hour on a bicycle and three hours in the study prepare more of a sermon than four hours in the study. Six days of work and one day of rest and worship mean more for humanity than seven days of secular interests. If you would keep the keen edge of efficiency on your mental powers, you must give time for rest and readjustment.

In our study of the forces that blunt the edge, we have found, by contrast, three positive rules for keeping the edge keen. First, use the axe; second, use it wisely; third, use it not too incessantly. Wise working and wise resting are among the essentials to continued efficiency.

It remains simply to mention a few other items in the list of what may be called "aids to keenness;" whetstones, so to speak, for the mental axe. Whether used or not, an axe not cared for tends to bluntness, a mind neglected tends to dullness.

Good reading is an aid to keenness. Reading in line with your work and reading out of line with your work. Reading which keeps you in touch with the times, and reading which brings the men and the nations of all times into your acquaintance. Reading the Bible, of which Charles Dudley Warner says, "It is the one book that no intelligent person who wishes to come in contact with the world of thought, and to share the ideas of the great minds of the Christian era, can afford to be ignorant of."

Good listening. You can pick for yourself the talking you will give attention to. There is the talking of the curbstone, of the barber shop, of the hotel corridor, of society, of the court room, of the lecture hall, of the church. Do your listening where helpful things are said.

Good seeing. Use the eyes for good books, good pictures, good everything. You are fortunate if you can travel and see the wonders of the world of nature and art and business. But as you walk along the city streets you have a choice of sights. You can see the loathsome allurement of the bill-boards, or the ennobling panorama of sky and leaf and flower. Open your eyes to the things that are worth seeing.

Good thinking. Meditation on that which is best sharpens the mind in all its powers. "Whatsoever things are true, whatsoever things are honorable, whatsoever things are just, whatsoever things are pure, whatsoever things are lovely, whatsoever things are of good report; if there be any virtue, and if there be any praise, think on these things."

The woodchopper and his axe offer some helpful truths for us all tonight, and particularly for you who are closing the public school days.

Some of you—I hope very many of you—are going on with your studies at college or university. Some of you close your years of study with the ending of this year's work. Whatever your plans for the future may be, as you are gathered here you are the possessors of the two factors essential to success. You have now, I am sure, the purpose of heart to wield in the wisest way the tools of service. God has given you the axe—the brain and body and heart. God and your parents and your teachers and the public school system have put the keen edge of efficiency on all your powers.

For the future years, God is the constant factor. For richness of result, genuineness of service, depth of satisfaction, you must furnish the abiding purpose, and you must keep the axe's edge keen. By use, by wise use, by needed rest from use, by the help of all the aids available, it is your splendid duty and privilege to keep the powers of heart and brain unfailingly whetted to the keen edge of efficiency.

"If the iron be blunt, and one do not whet the edge, then must he put to more strength—or else lose the large result of his service ; but wisdom is profitable to direct."

Class Day

Central M. E. Church, Monday Evening, June 19, 1899

Invocation,   -   -   -   -   -   -   -   Rev. Hunt

President's Address.   -   -   -   -   -   Phil Hasty

Class History,   -   -   -   -   -   -   Bell Cady

Vocal Solo,   -   -   -   -   -   -   Mr. George Van Buren

Class Poem,   -   -   -   -   -   -   Mildred Moon

Class Prophecy.   -   -   -   -   -   Constance Bement

Vocal Solo,   -   -   -   Mr. George Van Buren

Commencement Exercises

At Baird's Opera House, Wednesday Evening, June 21, 1899

Orchestra.
Invocation, ...   Rev. E. B. Allen
Orchestra.
Remarks, ...   Supt. S. B. Laird
Orchestra.
Oration, ...   Mildred Koonsman
Vocal Solo,   .   .   Anna McNeil Robson
Oration, ...   Arthur Reasoner
Vocal Solo, ...   Gage Christopher
Address, ...   Russel Ostrander
Remarks,   .   .   .   President Campbell
Remarks to Class, ...   Principal Holmes
Presentation of Diplomas.
Song, "America."
Benediction.

The Juniors by a Junior

Three years of that struggle to gain the final departure from the High School have passed away. Yet one would hardly think so if he were to listen to a Senior tell the blunders of the Juniors. Although the Seniors rejoice in criticising Juniors from September until May, they meekly come around and ask the Juniors to contribute to the Oracle.

Junior contributions were not sought for so eagerly until last year. Then it was that one of the greatest poets that ever lived was a member of the class of 1900. The present Senior class watched this class very closely, and finally decided that the best way to get the members interested was to give them representatives on the Oracle board. This was done, and two would-be Senior presidents were elected. There is no doubt but that the member who has been showing so much of his theatrical ability is longing to be editor-in-chief of the Oracle of 1900.

The fact that the Juniors are in possession of two of the greatest artists that ever entered the High School shows that they will have one of the finest illustrated Oracles ever published. [Ed.—With the exception of '99.]

In mentioning the good qualities of the Juniors it would be altogether improper to omit the name of Mr. O. L. Dane. Mr. Dane prides himself in his ability to manage receptions. The greatest trouble with Mr. Dane is that he finds it impossible to attend the receptions arranged for by himself. Anyone desiring the latest thing in music would do well to call on Miss Chapin for some of the new selections she has been playing in the assembly room. Taking the Junior class as a whole, it will make one of the best Senior classes that ever entered the Senior room.

With Mr. Lisle Smith as editor-in-chief, Miss Ostrander illustrator, Miss Dix at the head of the literary department, and Mr. Dane bill poster, our Oracle must succeed.

Ed.—We have but little to say about the above article. It was written by a Junior who has his eyes and ears wide open, and we are of the opinion that some of the sayings here recorded are likely to come true. We withhold the gentleman's name by special request.

Third Book of Chronicles

(Continued from the ORACLE of '98.)

Sept. 6, 1898. And behold, on this day all the tribes did assemble at the Temple of Learning.

Sept. 8. Then Rev. Thompson did give the assembly advice.

Sept. 15. And Rev. Swift did appear before the multitude to speak unto them.

Sept. 30. On this day all the tribes were assembled to shake the hands of the strangers.*

Oct. 1. O, Owosso! Great is thy shame; for our foot ball team did meet thee in battle, and the score of our victory was 27 to 0.

Oct. 5. And Miss Douglas did journey to a far country, and abode there that day.

Oct. 6. Behold, in the morning, Ernestine did raise her voice in praise.

Oct. 7. Lo, all complained of their unjust (?) rewards with which the overseers did reward them.

Oct. 11. And Supt. Hammond did proclaim the mighty works of Blair before the wise.

Oct. 12. Now all the tribes did rejoice because of their liberty from sunrise until sunset.

Oct. 15. Lo, the mighty did vanquish the Freshman tribe in battle.†

Oct. 19. And the chief did call an assembly of the Senior tribe.

Oct. 21. On this day at about the third hour of the afternoon the Senior tribe did begin to afflict the assembly with their words.

Oct. 24. A voice was heard—"Let there be silence throughout the tribe!"

Oct. 25. And Guy did read from the Holy Book, to the assembly of the wise, for the last time.

Oct. 26. Then women from a hostile tribe did advise economy in all things, and severe plainness of dress.

Oct. 28. Lo, the Junior tribe did proclaim a reception for the Freshman tribe, and the Freshmen did stand out in the rain, for the Juniors opened not the portals unto them.

Nov. 18. And Mr. McClure did show forth the mighty deeds of Lafayette.

Nov. 21. Behold, a new teacher did appear before the wise.

Nov. 23. There was weeping among the multitude because of their great sorrow‡; yet there was also great rejoicing because of the approaching day.§

* New teachers. † Ball game. ‡ Mr. Stewart's departure. § Thanksgiving.

Nov. 28.   And the tribes did reassemble at the Temple of Learning.

Dec. 2.   A mighty man‡ from a far country did address the multitude.

Dec. 21.   And on this day one band of brothers did assemble for merry-making.

Dec. 23.   And there was great joy among the frequenters of the Temple of Learning because of a fortnight's pleasure.

Dec. 27.   Lo, another band of brothers did proclaim a feast day.

Jan. 9, 1899.   And when the wise did assemble at the Temple of Learning they were sore dismayed by a new teacher.*

Jan. 30.   And behold, there was much wailing by reason of exams.

Feb. 6.   On this day the Senior tribe did set forth upon their last journey.

Feb. 16.   Lo, Ernestine did entertain a fair youth.

Feb. 21.   And all the tribes were sent forth from the Temple for one day's sojourn in the land of pleasure.

Mar. 3.   And the Senior tribe did begin to repeat their affliction of the multitude.

Mar. 7.   Behold, Rev. Bard did appear before the mighty with words of wisdom.

Mar. 9.   Rev. Swift did admonish the assembled tribes, to their edification.

Mar. 18.   Lo, all the overseers did journey to a city, afar off, and did return with strange ideas.

Mar. 21.   And more groans did sound forth because of examinations.

March 21.   That youth known as Charles Hayden did visit the Temple.

And there was great rejoicing because of another season of pleasure·

April 3.   And the tribes did once more gather at the Temple of Learning.

Apr. 7.   On this day the Junior tribe did appear before the multitudes in disguise,† and some did make speeches, and did lay great "Plans."

Apr. 10.   For many days a youth hath visited a Senior damsel, known as Miss Renner.

And Miss Dresser did become weary with climbing, and sat down on the topmost step of the topmost stairway of the Temple of Learning.

Apr. 13.   And Rev. Hunt did raise his voice before the multitude.

Apr. 14.   On this day Overseer Willey did excommunicate a youth, called Purvis, and a maiden, known as Yakeley, from Chemistry class.

Apr. 17.   Then came Clarence, the great Chief, among the wise, and the people listened to his voice. And he spake and said: "Forsake not the assembling of yourselves together on the coming Friday, as ye have done in times past."

Apr. 18.   Behold, four students from a distant college did visit us.

Apr. 21.   Lo, Miss Young did have company and did not diligently study the Algebra, to her hurt.

Apr. 24.   And in the morning the poet appeared, and lo! she was silent, neither would she speak aloud to the questions of the multitude.

Apr. 25.   On that day came forth Herr Smith with an exceedingly infinitesimal collar, and the Seniors did much long for opera glasses with which to observe it.

On that day did Clarence come again into the assembly of the wise and say: "Mead, except thou writest, thou shalt no longer abide in the assembly of the scribes," and he departed from among the people.

Apr. 26.   Miss Eberhart appeared with a white band bound about her head, for one of her eyes was injured by straining to see the collar of the said Herr Smith.

* Mr. Laird.   † Junior Ex.

I

Apr. 27. Mr. Brant returned again to the Temple of Learning, and the marks of the plague were yet upon his countenance.*

And Miss King did come before the great assembly and did read from the Holy Book.

Apr. 29. The Base Ball giants did journey to Eaton Rapids and were sore defeated.

May 1. And again the voice sounded—"Let all the tribe keep silence!"

May 2. And High Law Giver Willey did lead a company of the inquirers after knowledge down into the city to behold the great machines which do make light; and the hair of the company did stand on end.

May 3. Then came great ones from a far country and all the people did rush with one accord to the chief places of the city to observe them and to touch their hands.

May 4. And Miss Robinson said unto the Senior English classes, "Be ye diligent and ye shall go forth without questioning."†

May 6. And behold our team did sorely-defeat the Owosso giants.

May 9. In the morning Clarence said unto some of the Senior tribe, "You shall come up into a large place‡ and I will teach you to add to, to take from, to multiply and to divide."

May 10. And Miss Bement did ride out in her chariot with four other maidens of her tribe. And she did see a maiden whom she thought to be Miss Smith, from a neighboring tribe, wheeling a wheelbarrow. She did much long to ride therein, and called to the maiden and said, "Will ye not take me for a ride?" And lo! it was not Miss Smith, but a maid from some barbarian tribe whom Miss Bement knew not.

May 11. And one of the Senior girls did say unto the others of the tribe, "Arise and put hats on your heads and ten pieces of copper in your scrip, and let us go down into the city where much food is sold§ and there will we eat this noon." And they arose to the number of twenty-seven and did go with her. And when they had partaken of the repast they did gather at the portal and prepare to give the war-cry of the tribe. And two of the tribe did turn traitors and went apart saying, "We will not be counted among you."

May 12. And the wise from a neighboring tribe did come into our presence.

May 19. Great numbers from a more distant tribe did visit us. And on this day, also, the assembly did dissolve for a season to welcome Company E.

May 23. Rev. Osborne did lift up his voice in the midst of the mighty.

May 26-27. On these days the giants did contend at Ann Arbor.

May 29. On this day did the great chief, Clarence, promise to the Oracle an article on "Punctuality"; and he did much vex the Oracle Board by his tardiness.

June 9. And the Senior tribe did cease from their labors.

June 18. Rev. Swift did admonish and warn the multitude.

June 19. And chosen persons did look backward and forward and did tell us what they saw

June 20. The Junior tribe did assemble for their feast.

June 21. And all the Seniors did receive their rewards on this day.

June 22. The tribes did journey forth for a day's sojourn by the sea-side.

June 23. And the Senior tribe did dissolve, and the members did go to the north and to the south, to the east and to the west, and the places that knew them knew them no more.

Thus endeth the third book.

—

*German measles.   † Examinations.   ‡ Large assembly room.   § Donsereaux's Lunch Counter.

Grinds

AGNES JONES in English History. They could not become citizens until they were neutralized.

Seen on a General History examination paper. "The transmigration of soles."

DRAKE MEADE in English XII. "Did Pope write the Iliad and Odyssey?"

ED. FLANDERS (Reading). "Carve on every tree
The fair, the chaste, the unexpensive (unexpressive) she."

MISS LOTT. "Evidently you have not had much experience."

The Spanish fleet advanced on England in the shape of a chestnut.

GRACE ALLEN, German XI. "A long fire-red beard hung down over his breast and was fastened in three places to the marble table."

DRAKE MEADE, English XII. "To take his own advice Bacon should be 'chewed and digested.'"

English XII. "Satan and his companions were condemned to internal punishment."

MR. HOLMES, Geology. "'Arcadian rock' makes one think of Tennyson's Evangeline."

A Senior dropped one of the large dictionaries and was heard to exclaim, "O what a fall was there, my countrymen; then 'u' and 'i' and all of 'us' fell down!"

Cæsar Class. "They all threw themselves at Cæsar's weeping feet."

MISS DOUGLAS. "Why did the people of India think that a soul passing into an elephant went more directly to Bramah than from any other animal?"

VICTOR GARDNER. "I don't know, unless the elephant was larger and so had more of Bramah in him."

MR. SMITH in Algebra. "Miss Young, which does x equal, cows or sheep?"

MISS YOUNG. "Oxen."

Wanted Oct. 19, '98, a hair dresser. Enquire Henry Jones.

DRAKE MEADE. "Can the prisoners vote?"

MISS SMITH. "No, not while they are serving their term of office."

MISS DOUGLAS. "Why was King —— hurrying back to Persia?"

"To kill Smerdis again."

FRITZ GRESLEY. "An axiom is a truth assumed to be self accident."

MISS ATKINS. "And Venus the mother himself."

MARGARET FORRESTER in General History. "Isn't Sparta somewhere near Greece?"

MARY BAILEY in England IX. "A poem of four lines is a quadruped."

MR. STEWART, illustrating the pendulum, suspends a yard stick from the gas jet and says: "There is a place in this stick which when I strike it, both stick and string will swing together." He strikes it and the string and stick unexpectedly part company, and the stick hits Mr. Tracy.

MR. STEWART. "I think that must have been the place, but I did n't get the reading."

MR. HOLMES. "What do we get from Bermuda? That is a subject that will bring tears to our eyes."

MISS ROBINSON. "Define a chair."

MERLE URQUHART. "Four legs, a back, intended for *two*."

MR. STEWART. "Take a bottled-up cork— what 's the matter?"

MR. STEWART. later. "Why can't you pull a pail full the water out? I 'm not Dutch."

DEAKE MEADE. English XII. "Who steals my purse steals cash."

MR. STEWART in Physics. "It will be a rather *homely* illustration, but suppose you take two people built like Mr. Hedges and myself."

ADELBERT BAKER, English XII. "Milton thought marriage was a failure."

MISS ROBINSON. "He didn't seem to be discouraged."

MR. DEMEREST. "A convex polygon is one that has none of its surface inside of the perimeter."

MISS DOUGLAS. "What are the divisions of the human race?"

MARIAN MALTBY. "Ancient, medieval, and modern."

MISS D. "What are the divisions of history?"

MISS M. "Black, white, and yellow."

MISS ATKINS in Greek Class. "Give a good English translation."

MILTON CAINE. "They followed not because they had chosed but because they knew he was capable."

MISS ATKINS (consulting the dictionary). "Why, here are so many words!!!!"

In Cicero. "No one to 'lamitate' the destruction of the great empire."

MR. FORESTER. "Demosthenes went in a cave and studied to be an oratory."

MISS ATKINS. "Translate 'Quid est in templo.' "

ORLANDO BARNES. "What woman does not love her children?"

MISS SMITH. "Where did the English troops go during the first part of the Revolution?"

FRED DORSEY. "To Halifax."

"He was sent to Troy in the arms of his fatherland." Virgil.

Virgil. "The old man put on his shoulders."

ARTHUR REASONER, in Virgil. "She hangs upon his lips when he speaks."

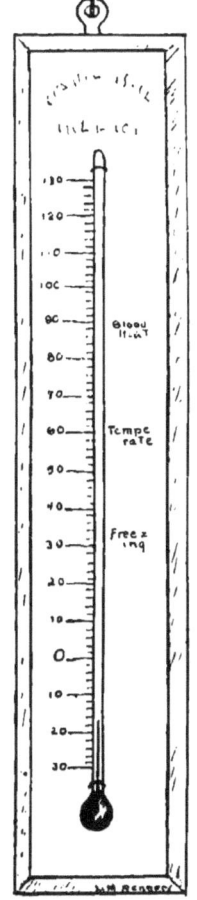

Class Spirit.

CHAS. HOWARD. "As soon as the slaves were freed they went mad."

MISS ATKINS. "He was immortal and didn't die."

MISS ATKINS. "Mr. Hartness may read."

MR. HARTNESS. "Thus the fates decreed." This was the end of the lesson.

MISS DOUGLAS. "What is the Koran?"

MISS PARMELEE. "The Old Testament."

MARIE NICHOLS, working in the Physical Laboratory. "Helen, are your feet just like Jessie's?"

MISS LOTT. "What were the direct cause of Sumner's death?"

FRESHIE. "Why, he married and—"

MR. SMITH. "A book was lost last yesterday."

NED HOPKINS, in Virgil. "The hired mourners were generally women and they raised a great rumpus."

MABEL C. "She heard the sun shine."

ORACLE BOARD. "Do editors ever do wrong?" "No." "What do they do?" "They do write."

DRAKE MEADE, describing "The Cotter's Saturday Night." "The cotter's wife stands smiling in the doorway with a 'wee bit ingle blinkin' bonnily' in her arms!" "Wee bit ingle"- grate fire.

MR. WILLEY. "Take a solid glass tube."

MR. WILLEY, in Physics Class, holds up a cake tin three inches deep, changed into a heat-testing apparatus, and explains, "This was a *pie*-tin once."

Feb. 9, Miss Lamb was guilty of slang. "The rough peasant's dress led him to suppose that a peasant girl was 'in it.'"

Proposed declension of "du:"

Correct—	The way it was given—
Du	Do
Deiner	Dinah
Dir	Dear
Dich	Do

HAROLD HEDGES in Grammar. "A 'Goatie' is a little goat."

FLORENCE GREEN in Grammar. "'Ugliness' is common and abstract."

EDITH DAVIS. "The opposite of step-son is step-cousin."

In English Class. "Johnson went to London with 'Irene' in his pocket." Large pockets must have been one of his peculiarities.)

Woman leads the world. She used smoke-less powder for ages before man thought of inventing it.—Ex.

Women are not as considerate as men. Frequently men who occupy the front seats at the theater don't even wear hair.—Ex.

Some jokes should be printed on thin paper so that the reader could see through them.—Ex.

Train up a hired girl in the way she should go, and the first thing you know she's gone.- -Ex.

It is said that banana peels make good slippers.—Ex.

The full dress suit often covers an empty stomach.—Ex.

Truth is mighty- -at least mighty scarce.—Ex.

You can't judge a man's character by the high standing of his collar. -Ex.

In ancient times the people multiplied on the face of the earth; but now they use slates.---Ex.

A man who breaks his word is not necessarily a liar—perhaps he stutters.—Ex.

The devil probably told Eve that apples were good for the complexion. Ex.

Thunder—the only reliable weather report yet discovered.—Ex.

Love may be blind, but the neighbors generally have their eyes open.—Ex.

It may not be proper to precede the father of your best girl down the stairs—but sometimes you have to.—Ex.

The wise virgins of the olden time kept their lamps trimmed and burning; those of the present generation keep the gas turned low.—Ex.

About the worst joke a woman can play on a man is to marry him.—Ex.

The State of Matrimony is one of the United States, even if it isn't on the map.--Ex.

There is no law to prohibit fighting in the State of Matrimony.—Ex.

The busy little boot-black never fails to improve each shining hour.—Ex.

The easiest thing for a boy to catch with a bent pin is the school teacher.—Ex.

A man never has real trouble until he has a son to wear his clothes.—Ex.

Coxey's Barber Shop   Five Chairs
First-Class Work
Guaranteed   Forrest W. Wilcox, Proprietor

CLOTHING DEPARTMENT, at

A. M. Donsereaux's Department Store

... SPECIALTIES ...

BOYS' AND CHILDREN'S SUITS—in all the leading styles of each season.
We can equip the boy from 3 to 19 years of age, in the latest style and best fabrics,
at lower prices than any other store in the city. Everything in the Furnishing
Goods Line that a boy or youth can want.

We have put forth a great effort in purchasing our line of

... Men's Clothing ...

for Fall, and intend to have the very best line of Suits and Overcoats in this
market.

Don't worry; but if you really must worry, try and worry some one else. Ex.

Don't waste your time in disputing figures; they seldom lie except in gas meters.—Ex.

Don't mistake your calling. If you have brains, go into business; if you haven't, go into society. Ex.

When a woman marries a man she not only takes his name, but nearly everything else the poor devil possesses.—Ex.

Language is called the mother-tongue because the father seldom gets a chance to use it.—Ex.

A wife is called the better half because she usually gets the better of the other half.—Ex.

The father of twins usually finds marriage a howling success.—Ex.

After man came woman, and she has been after him ever since.—Ex.

... COURSE OF STUDY FOR THE ...

LANSING CITY SCHOOLS

APPROVED SEPTEMBER, 1897

♪ ♪ ♪

HIGH SCHOOL COURSES OF STUDY

	CLASSICAL.	LATIN.	SCIENTIFIC.	ENGLISH.
NINTH YEAR.	Latin.	Latin.	Latin.	Latin or German or Phys. Geo.
	Algebra.	Algebra.	Algebra.	Algebra.
	History.	History. U. S.	History. U. S.	History, U. S.
	English.	English.	English.	English.
	Latin.	Latin.	Latin.	Latin or German or Physiology.
	Algebra.	Algebra.	Algebra.	Algebra.
	Botany.	Botany.	Botany.	Botany.
	English.	English.	English.	English.
TENTH YEAR.	Latin.	Latin.	Latin.	Latin or German or Eng. Gram.
	Algebra.	Algebra.	Algebra.	Algebra.
	General History.	General History.	General History.	General History.
	English.	English.	English.	English.
	Latin.	Latin.	Latin.	Latin or German or Bookkeeping.
	Arithmetic.	Arithmetic.	Arithmetic.	Arithmetic.
	General History.	General History.	General History.	General History.
	English.	English.	English.	English.
ELEVENTH YEAR.	Latin.	Latin.	German.	Geometry.
	Geometry.	Geometry.	Eng. Grammar.	Chemistry.
	Greek.	German.	Chemistry.	English History.
	English.	English.	English.	English.
	Latin.	Latin.	German.	Geometry.
	Geometry.	Geometry.	Chemistry.	Chemistry.
	Greek.	German.	Civil Government	English History.
	English.	English.	English.	English.
TWELFTH YEAR.	Latin.	Latin.	German.	English.
	Physics.	Physics.	Geometry.	Physics.
	Greek.	German.	Physics.	Political Econ.
	English.	English.	English.	Reviews.
	Latin.	Latin.	German.	English.
	Physics.	Physics.	Geometry.	Physics.
	Greek.	German.	Physics.	Civil Government
	English.	English.	English.	Reviews.

English three periods a week, all other studies five.

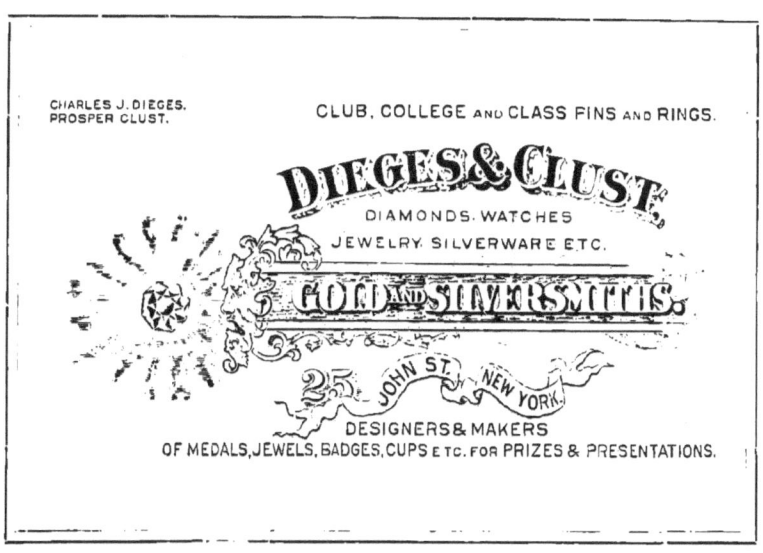
See Editorials of Oracle for
'99's Opinion of Mr. Le Clear's Work.